CHOKE

Other Books by Obert Skye

Beyond Foo, Book 1: Geth and the Return of the Lithens

The Creature from My Closet, Book 1: Wonkenstein

Leven Thumps and the Gateway to Foo

Leven Thumps and the Whispered Secret

Leven Thumps and the Eyes of the Want

Leven Thumps and the Wrath of Ezra

Levan Thumps and the Ruins of Alder

Pillage

*Professor Winsnicker's Book of Proper Etiquette
for Well-Mannered Sycophants*

CHOKE

OBERT SKYE

Illustrations by Owen Richardson

SHADOW
MOUNTAIN

This book is a work of fiction. The characters, places, and incidents in it are the product of the author's imagination or are represented fictitiously.

First printing in hardbound 2010
First printing in paperbound 2011

Visit us at ShadowMountain.com

Library of Congress Cataloging-in-Publication Data
Skye, Obert.
    Choke / Obert Skye; illustrated by Owen Richardson.
        p.   cm.
    Summary: Using his renowned lack of common sense, sixteen-year-old Beck Phillips gets himself and his friends Kate and Wyatt embroiled in more dragon adventures, as they discover and hatch the last remaining dragon stone.
    ISBN 978-1-60641-653-2 (hardbound : alk. paper)
    ISBN 978-1-60908-772-2 (paperbound)
    1. Fantasy fiction, American.   2. Children's stories, American.
[1. Dragons—Fiction.   2. Magic—Fiction.   3. Blessing and cursing—Fiction.
4. Eccentrics and eccentricities—Fiction.   5. Uncles—Fiction.]   I. Richardson, Owen, ill.   II. Title.
    PZ7.S62877Cho 2010
    [Fic]—dc22   2010001628

Printed in the United States of America
R. R. Donnelley, Crawfordsville, IN

10   9   8   7   6   5   4   3   2   1

Contents

CHAPTER 1: Under Great Pressure 1

CHAPTER 2: Doing Alright 11

CHAPTER 3: Really White Man......................... 32

CHAPTER 4: I'm Going Slightly Mad 46

CHAPTER 5: It Is Late 60

CHAPTER 6: In Just Seven Days 70

CHAPTER 7: Don't Lose Your Head 80

CHAPTER 8: Good Company 95

CHAPTER 9: Blurred Vision 108

CHAPTER 10: Rock It 132

CHAPTER 11: Don't Stop Me 143

CHAPTER 12: Life Is Pretty Real 151

CHAPTER 13: Father to Son 158

CHAPTER 14: Rain Must Fall 169

CHAPTER 15: The White Queen 178

CHAPTER 16: She Makes Me 190

CHAPTER 17: Liar 200

CHAPTER 18: Is This the World They Created? 209

CHAPTER 19: Misfire 218

CHAPTER 20: Action Right Now 237

CHAPTER 21: Put Out the Fire........................... 251

CHAPTER 22: Waiting for the Hammer to Fall............. 260

CHAPTER 23: Stone Cold Wacko 268

CHAPTER 24: Keep Yourself Alive 277

CHAPTER 25: The Dragon Attack 285

CHAPTER 26: Another One Bites the Dust 294

CHAPTER 27: Was It All Worth It? 318

CHAPTER 28: Flash 324

"Oops?" he said, repeating what I had just said. "Oops?"

"Sorry," I tried.

"It was done," he mourned. "It was over."

"I didn't mean to," I apologized. "Honest."

"You didn't mean to what?" he asked sternly, towering over me, the ends of his long nightshirt billowing lightly. "You didn't mean to find the stone among the millions of stones?"

"Well . . ."

"You didn't mean to then plant the stone?" he continued, not even giving me a second to answer.

"I . . ."

"It was by mistake that you harvested it?" he said scornfully. "And then, quite by accident, that you raised it and let it loose?"

"Well, when you put it that way, it does sort of make me look bad."

My dad massaged his forehead as if there were a tattoo there he was hoping to rub off.

"Beck," he sighed.

"Dad," I said manipulatively.

"This is on your head," he whispered. "What the queen pillages will be the work of her talons and your hands."

I looked at my hands, marveling at all the trouble they were capable of getting me into.

CHAPTER 1

Under Great Pressure

THE FIELD ON THE EDGE OF Callowbrow was filled and students of all shapes and sizes milling around, trying not to look as self-conscious as so many students often did. Callowbrow itself had been torn apart by the dragons, but now many of the repairs were well underway or completed. The school was beginning to look like itself again—the dark bricks jutted out of the green fields and pushed up into the misty sky like scaly beasts. Low clouds crowned the roofs and the high-climbing roses that peppered many of the walls and towers.

I walked quickly through the milling students, holding one end of a very heavy duffel bag. The other end was being carried by Kate. She had reluctantly agreed to help me with what I was

1

calling an "experiment." I had invited Wyatt to join us, but he had to stay in the library and do some make-up work.

Kate and I pushed through the students and up to a free-standing shop shed. The door was unlocked, and we slipped in unnoticed. I closed and bolted the door behind us. I could still hear students doing student-like things outside. I set the weighty bag on the ground and unzipped the long zipper.

"What is it, Beck?" Kate asked.

"I think it's some sort of huge ball."

"Someone gave it to you?"

"Kind of," I answered.

We pulled it out of the bag and unfolded part of it.

"We need to lift it up and spread it open," I said, tugging at the thick material.

"It's huge," Kate said with awe. "Not to mention incredibly heavy."

"Baby," I replied, slightly out of breath. "Listen, if you wanna leave, have at it. The door's right there."

I flipped my head back, pointing to the door.

"No way," Kate whispered. "Someone needs to keep an eye on what you're doing."

I smiled, unfolding the thick material further.

"Wyatt should be here," she added.

"I know. I feel bad for him, missing all this fun."

"You're crazy, Beck, you know that," Kate added. "Absolutely crazy."

I looked down at my hands and thought about what Kate had just said. My hands didn't look crazy. They looked like normal sixteen-year-old-boy hands. And I didn't feel crazy. I mean I should have known better, but that was usually the case.

It's sad, really. You'd think that a sixteen-year-old boy with brown eyes, dark hair, and a mischievous smile, who had lost his mother, been shipped across country to live with his crazy uncle (only to learn he could make things grow and bring dragons to life), and practically ruined an entire town, would know better than to go messing around with things that could cause further amounts of trouble.

"What's the matter?" Kate asked.

"Nothing," I said, looking up. "Here, give me that air hose. There's a nozzle here."

Kate handed me the thick black hose with the large metal tip. I shoved it into the dusty plastic hole on the bottom of the material. The air hose slowly slipped into the opening, chirping like a sick dolphin. Once in, the two plastic parts seemed to bond, making it impossible for me to pull it back out. I tugged as hard as I could.

"Cool," I said, smiling. "It fits perfectly."

Kate continued to unfold the large cloth ball. "You're going to blow it up in here?"

"There's plenty of room," I assured her.

We were in the small shop shed that our school used to teach shop. It was old and sat at the far end of the neatly groomed soccer field. It was one of the few buildings that had not been damaged by the dragons as they had picked apart the town of Kingsplot and, more specifically, the campus of Callowbrow. The shed was relatively empty, with tools lining the walls and a welding tank in the far corner. Near the door was a large air compressor with two silver tanks.

It was the air compressor I had come for.

Two days ago, while searching through a dusty room in the manor I live in, I found an old wooden trunk. After accidentally breaking the lock on the trunk, I stumbled upon what I thought was a massive folded blanket. I was wrong. It wasn't a blanket. It was a huge folded ball. It was made of red velvet with orange stripes running down it and a valve at the bottom. I thought it was a pretty interesting discovery, but I felt like it would be an even more interesting find once it was blown up. I figured I would blow it up, roll it out of the large doors of the shed, and then all of us at Callowbrow could mess around with it. It seemed like it would make for a fun-filled afternoon. So, I had smuggled the ball to school in a huge black duffel bag. At that point, I recruited Kate to help me fill it with air.

"This is dumb," Kate said. "This is another one of your dumb ideas."

I smiled at Kate—she didn't smile back. I was okay with that. She still looked just fine, what with her long, red hair and deep blue eyes. Her skin was pale—like two-percent milk—and she was wearing her school uniform, which consisted of a plaid skirt, white shirt, and white knee socks.

She was pretty, but I was in no mood to tell her that.

"I'm not doing this," she insisted, but still making no move to leave.

I smiled. "I think you are. Besides, it will be cool. The school will talk about this for years."

"That's what I'm afraid of."

"It's going to be fun," I said with my most convincing voice.

I flipped the switch and the compressor began to whirl and moan. It was loud and pulsating, the thump of it bouncing off the shed walls and pounding my ears.

"It's loud!" Kate yelled.

"I know," I hollered back.

The thick fabric of the ball began to puff up. A large fold pushed out, doubling the size of the material. Like a fat wad of velvety dough, the velvet ball began to swell.

"It's really big," Kate said needlessly.

She was right, but that was becoming a rather obvious detail. My heart started to race as the ball swelled. My life had been way too calm the past eight months. I could barely remember my life before Kingsplot. My mother, who had really been my aunt, was a memory I had to work on to bring into focus. Her death still hurt, but the sting wasn't as sharp or as clear as it had once been. And I was thrilled to have discovered my father, but, to be honest, the relationship had a lot of growing to do. He still lived on the top floor of the mansion and came down only when I pestered him. He claimed he knew nothing about raising a son. I agreed with him, but I was willing to help him learn. Two nights ago we had argued over bringing a TV into the huge manor.

"Just one," I had argued.

"Noise," was his clipped reply.

Truthfully, the gigantic manor I lived in could use a little more noise. It was still a huge, dark home with hundreds of locked rooms and winding halls with no one to walk its halls but me, Millie, Thomas, and Wane. But, as most adults do, my father had put up a wall and insisted the discussion was over without ever hearing me out. It was later that night that I discovered the ball. I think that's why I wasn't too worried about what was happening now, seeing how I could always argue that I never would have even found the ball if I had been safely watching TV.

The material of the ball pushed out again, a long fold popping open like six sleeping bags. My excitement began to feel like fear.

"I don't think it's just a ball!" Kate hollered.

The expanding ball was as wide as the shed and rapidly growing taller. I could only see Kate from the neck up now. I watched her scoot back to provide more room for the ball.

"Open the doors!" I yelled.

"I can't reach them," she yelled back. "Just turn it off!"

I reached down and hit the switch. The compressor began to scream even louder.

"Off," Kate yelled, as if I had misunderstood her the first time.

"I can't!"

The ball sprang open three more folds making it as large as the room. I couldn't see Kate. Actually, I couldn't see anything besides the material of the ball pushing into my face as it expanded even faster. I could hear Kate's muffled scream and the sound of someone violently rattling the doors to the shed trying to get in. I reached down to hit the switch again, but I could no longer reach it.

The ball pushed me up against the wall, lifting me off my

feet and scraping me up the wall. It expanded tightly against my chest and face. My head was forced to the side and crammed flat against the wall. I wanted to yell, "I'm sorry," to Kate, but the moment didn't seem right, and my lungs were completely compressed.

The ball expanded even further, stealing any room for my lungs to expand. I was stuck to the wall, my feet inches from the floor. Velvet was pushing into my nose and the ball was smothering me.

I tried to kick and hit, but my arms and legs were pinned against the wall. My vision was nothing but a fading smudge, as bits of my life drifted across my mind like the fluid on the back of my eyelids. I could see my father, Aeron, and Millie. I could see two Kates, the happy one and one that was going to wring my neck if and when we survived.

"I thought this would be fun," I yelled, unable to fully move my mouth. "I'm going to die."

There was no air, and the pressure was so painful I could feel my blood being squeezed from the top half of my body and down into my toes. The air compressor was squealing and hissing so loudly that if a genie had appeared and granted me three wishes, at least one of them would be that I could close my ears.

I should have at least closed my eyes.

Just when I thought I was going to die from suffocation, a noise unlike any I had heard before—and I had heard dragons fighting and towns being torn apart—ripped through my head. Wind raced over me and I could feel a tremendous pain in my head as I flew backward and into a misty, blinding darkness.

Illustration from page 1 of The Grim Knot

CHAPTER 2

Doing Alright

I COULD HEAR THE SOUND OF SLOW, heavy rain hitting against a roof above me—it sounded like fat water balloons exploding in slow motion. My eyes were shut and my head felt like a heavy brick of clay. I could hear someone or something shuffling around me.

I strained and opened my left eye.

Just so you know, I'm never happy to wake up. I'm even less happy about it when I wake up with tubes sticking out of my arms and a large woman with a thick moustache and floppy ears is standing over me saying, "Awake are you?" She sounded like Yoda. Her breath was the smell of old cleaning spray and vinegar. I probably would have thought she was a witch if it weren't for the words "Nurse Agatha" stitched across the white hat she was wearing over her gray hair. She pushed a button on

11

the side of my bed and the top half rose so that I was sort of halfway sitting.

I moaned.

"Children like you fill the beds of those who really need it," she carped.

I shifted in my bed, opened my right eye, and looked down the long dreary hall. There were at least fifty beds lining the wall, and all of them were empty.

"What about all those beds?" I mumbled.

"Don't be smart," Nurse Agatha snipped while writing something down on a clipboard.

I was going to ask her if she wanted me to be dumb, but I could tell she wasn't in the mood for levity. I let my tired eyes roll over my surroundings. The hospital hall was made of stone walls and a glass ceiling with white metal veins holding the glass panels in place. Green ivy covered the edges. At the end of the row of beds there was a large desk with papers on it and a big yellow call button sticking out of the wall above it. On the other side were the double doors.

I turned my head to the left and saw a small potted plant with three red blooms in a clay pot on the table next to my bed. It looked like a mini bush with large delicate flowers. Partly hidden in the leaves was a small card stuck in the tines of a tiny plastic pitchfork that poked into the dirt. The card said, "Get well," in Millie's handwriting. The plant was the only spot of color in the whole room.

"Where is everyone?"

"If you mean your . . . relatives, I'm sure they'll be here soon."

The long silver hairs beneath Nurse Agatha's nose made me feel even sicker than I did.

"We'll notify them of your consciousness," she added.

"Thanks."

"Don't be telling me thanks," she scolded. "If you were my child I would have you locked up."

"Thanks," I said again, although with considerably less enthusiasm. "So Kate's all right?"

Nurse Agatha nodded her head. "No thanks to you, blowing up buildings like a criminal. You know I went to Calloway years ago. I took shop in that very shed."

"That school must be old," I said weakly, not really thinking about what I was saying.

"The campus deserves your respect," she continued. "All four walls of the shed were blown open. It was completely ruined. Three students were injured by flying bricks and the field is a mess. You're fortunate you didn't kill someone."

I didn't feel very fortunate.

"I didn't mean to ruin everything," I said honestly. "I

thought it was just a big ball. I didn't know it would grow so huge."

Nurse Agatha shook her head and walked to the end of my bed and put both of her hands on her hips. She had on a stiff, white dress covered by an even stiffer white apron. Her arms were flabby and when she moved they jiggled like soft rubber snakes. She looked straight at me, her old eyes burning through me like hot pokers. "You kids walk the streets of Kingsplot and chew your gum and light your matches and leave things worse for those who walk behind."

"Light our matches?" I asked, confused.

"You know what I mean," she snipped. "Don't sass me with your spoiled mouth."

I pictured my mouth being a big, rotten, mushy orange.

"Had I married and had children, they would have known discipline," she went on. "They'd know order."

"Lucky pretend kids," I said sarcastically.

"Bah," she said as if she were trying out for the part of Scrooge.

"Is it still Tuesday?" I asked, sitting up.

"If you mean next Tuesday it is," she groused.

"I've been asleep for a week?" I asked, sitting up even faster. My head swam and I could feel myself tipping toward her. She pushed me back as if I were a bothersome stranger leaning into her on the subway.

I lay back down. "What about Kate?"

"She's fine," Agatha said smugly. "She received only a few bruises and cuts. You're lucky it wasn't worse."

I tried to smile.

"I know about you," Nurse Agatha growled.

"You must know only the bad things," I said. I figured if she knew anything good she wouldn't be treating me so poorly.

"Is there anything else to know?" She smiled a cruel smile and breathed out. Her vinegar breath settled over me like a sticky cobweb. She looked at her clipboard intently. "You're the product of money and greed. You're the child who brought those . . . beasts to our peaceful town. You come from a family that's both bonkers and bewitched, and you have brought even me more trouble than I need."

I didn't know what to say. "Are you reading that off a chart?"

She slammed the clipboard down on the bed. "Fun is what you think you are. Well, I, for one, won't smile as long as you are roaming our streets."

I wondered if she had actually ever smiled at anytime or anywhere.

She pulled out a syringe and set it on the small table by my bed. The needle looked at least four inches long and as thick as a pencil.

"What's . . . ?"

She smiled. I wanted to point out that she had lied about never smiling at me, but I was distracted by the fact that she was dabbing rubbing alcohol on a cotton swab.

Her grin spread.

"Can't you put that stuff into my IV?" I asked with concern.

"Tough guy like you can handle the needle."

"Wait, I'm not really that tough," I tried. "Can't we wait for . . ."

Nurse Agatha was suddenly in the mood for action. She grabbed my left arm, jammed up my left sleeve, rubbed alcohol on me as if I were the world's most stubborn stain, and then picked up the syringe and shoved the needle into my arm before I could properly scream. As she pushed the needle in, I could feel my eyeballs rolling to the back of my head. She withdrew the needle, slapped—and I mean slapped—a Band-Aid onto my arm, yanked down my sleeve, and smiled again. For the record, her smile didn't make her any more attractive; her face kind of looked like a big, soft melon that too many people had stuck their fingers into.

"What was that for?" I complained.

"Just in case," she said.

"You don't like me, do you?"

"Here at Bleeding Heart Memorial we care for all our patients," she answered. "But, no. Ring the bell over there on the wall once if there's an emergency."

"I didn't mean to blow it up," I tried to tell her again. "I thought it was just a big ball."

Nurse Agatha walked off. Well, it was more like she creaked off, her bones making a horrible clicking noise as she moved.

I closed my eyes and breathed in deeply. When I opened them, it was still raining, and the light in the room hadn't shifted much. I looked up at the ivy outside the glass ceiling. I focused on it and tried to get it to move, but it didn't. Ever since the last dragon had been killed, my ability to make things grow had been spotty at best. I had spent a number of days in back of the manor helping Thomas manicure the overgrown gardens. But my ability had not shown up at all. In fact, weeds seemed to resist my pulling them out, and any pruning I did turned out ugly and sad. In the last few weeks it almost seemed as if the plants and trees were out to get me. I kept tripping over roots that weren't there before and finding large bits of dirty lettuce in some of my food. My father said there was nothing to worry about, and that it was all in my mind. But when I reminded him that that same mind had gotten me into a lot of trouble in the past, he said just to keep an eye on anything green.

I looked over to see the potted plant Millie had sent me. It wasn't there.

"That's weird."

I looked around, figuring that Nurse Agatha had moved it. I couldn't see it anywhere.

"She stole my plant," I complained to myself. "What kind of nurse steals her patient's plant?"

I flopped back down against my pillow, closed my eyes, and sighed. I wanted to go home. My head hurt a little, but other than that I felt fine, and I didn't want to spend another day here. I could hear Nurse Agatha coming back, her feet scraping against the floor.

"Did you come to return my plant?" I asked, keeping my eyes closed.

There was some more grating sounds, but no answer.

"I'm trying to meditate," I said sarcastically.

There was no reply. I opened my eyes and looked around. Nobody was there, the hall was empty and the sound of rain plinking off the glass above was the only noise I could hear. I closed my eyes again and tried to breathe easier. Click, click.

My eyelids sprang open. A machine next to my bed whirled and whizzed for a few seconds and then shuttered. I looked across the large room and wished the bell for me to ring for help was closer.

"It's just the noises of an old hospital," I whispered, trying to comfort myself. I closed my eyes and was just about to drift off again when I heard more clicking. I kept my eyes shut, reminding myself that it was just some old machine or vent.

Click, scrape.

The scraping noise was even less comforting. I wished I were knocked out or that I had some earplugs. I pretended the hospital had a helper dog and that he was the one making the noise. While I was busy pretending with my eyes closed, I felt a tug on my blanket. I was so surprised that I didn't react fast enough. The blanket was pulled down and off the edge of my bed.

"Nurse!" I yelled, sitting up. "Nurse!"

I looked at my bare legs. I glanced around the long, narrow room. I was alone. I made fun of myself for acting like such a baby. The blanket had obviously just slipped down off my bed.

"Stupid blanket."

I threw my legs over the side of the bed and sat up. The plastic tubing connected to my right arm was long enough for me to move a little. The room flashed bright from a bolt of lightning. It was followed directly by the roar of thunder.

"Perfect."

The rain began to fall with greater force upon the glass

ceiling. Lightning flashed again, and the lights in the hospital flickered out.

"Perfect," I complained. "What a lovely hospital."

The whole scene was now colored in gray, cloudy twilight. I stood up and walked to the edge of the hospital bed to get my blanket. It was sitting on the floor in a bunched-up pile. I pulled it up and climbed back into the bed. I thought about going over to the bell and ringing it, but in all honesty I really didn't want to see Nurse Agatha again.

As I laid down, lightning flashed, followed directly by a heavy crack of thunder. I tried to remember if buildings with glass and metal roofs were safe during a lightning storm. I told myself that glass was probably like rubber and lightning couldn't hurt it. It wasn't the truth, but it made me feel a little better.

Scrape, click, scrape.

My blanket began to slide down me again as my heart did likewise. This time I grabbed the blanket and pulled it back up and under my chin.

It slid some more.

I jerked it up, but there was resistance. I figured it was just snagged on part of the bed. I yanked harder, and it yanked back. I should have taken a moment to realize that something wasn't right, but instead I just kept pulling. The only thing I could think of was that my blanket was caught in part of the bed's electrical system. The blanket pulled back, causing me to sit up. I wrapped my hands around my end of it and leaned backward. I was playing tug-of-war with my blanket and losing. I heaved, and the blanket hoed. I was wrenched up and forward, my body falling face-first onto the end of the bed. I could see the white tile floor. I could also see that I was completely wrong about my blanket having been caught in the electrical part of my bed. There was something green and growling down below.

"What the . . . ?"

I tried to drag the blanket up, but my position was bad, and I fell off the end of the bed and down onto the tiled floor. The tube popped out of my arm, and my right shoulder hit part of the blanket. I attempted to roll over so that I could get on my feet and run away. My attempt was thwarted by something heavy and hard smacking me directly in the forehead. I was snapped down flat, the back of my head hitting the floor. I looked up as I lay on the floor, and I could see that the potted plant Millie had sent me was sitting on my forehead. My breathing was labored, and the pot felt heavy. I really didn't know what to do. I had been a Boy Scout briefly when I lived in Chicago, so I had learned a few knots and how to whittle before I caused some trouble and was asked to join another troop. But in those two months, I never learned what to do if a houseplant had just head-butted you.

I rolled my eyes back and looked up at the pot. The plant leaned forward. It was wriggling and lowering itself closer to my face. If I weren't a rational human being, I would have sworn that the three bloodred flowers were grinning sinisterly at me.

The largest bloom cocked its head, pulled back a few inches, and then lunged at my nose. It clamped on and dug its thistle-like leaves into my skin.

I tried to scream, but the second flower jammed itself into my mouth and grabbed hold of my tongue.

I chomped down, hoping to bite the bloom off and free my tongue but I was too slow. All I did was bite down hard on my tongue.

"Owwhaaahaaaah!"

I thrashed violently, rolling over onto my side and bucking the plant and its pot away from my head. I got on my hands and knees and looked toward where the plant had been. It was lying on its side and rolling back and forth. It rocked and then flipped itself up. I stayed on all fours, watching in disbelief as it hopped closer.

Click, click.

The biggest flower bent down and chomped on the card Millie had written—grinding its petals together as if they were teeth and tearing the card into shreds. As it was chewing, the second flower wrapped itself around the plastic pitchfork that had held the card and yanked it out of the dirt. It whipped back and let it fly straight at me. The tiny tines jabbed my arm, drawing blood. The plant clicked closer.

I scrambled to stand as fast as I could. I'm not proud of what happened next, but I started to run. I ran from that houseplant like a small child running from a huge tiger. I also sounded like one—a small child, not a tiger.

"Heeeeeeeeeeellllllp!"

The plant whipped its clay pot around like a tail and threw itself into my legs. I tripped and went flying in between an empty bed and a tall counter. I crabwalked myself against the wall while trying to catch my breath. The plant righted itself and turned to look at me. All three flowers were bristling and moving. They clicked the thorns on their stems together and lurched forward balancing on the bottom front base of the pot. The pot rolled a couple of inches to the right and then rolled toward the left. Back and forth, back and forth—slowly getting closer.

"Stop!" I tried to command it, knowing that, in the past, growing things had obeyed me. "Freeze."

It rolled nearer.

"Nurse!"

Lightning struck, illuminating the grey room. The rabid plant looked like some sort of foliage zombie under strobe lights as it moved even closer—back and forth, back and forth.

I could see a tall bottle on the counter next to me. I picked up the bottle and waved it in the direction of the plant.

"Get away!"

The plant stopped and rocked back, resting on the entire base of its pot.

"I'm serious," I yelled.

Apparently it didn't believe me.

Click, click, click.

I didn't know what to do; it was now only about ten feet away. I slammed the bottle down against the counter, breaking the bottom off and giving me a jagged weapon. Small bits of glass chimed down against the floor.

"Get back!"

The plant stopped, and all three flowers cocked their heads as if to get a better look at the broken bottle in my hand.

"Yeah," I said breathing hard. "And I'll use it."

The storm exploded all over the room. "Now," I panted. "Go back."

The plant shivered and bent forward so that all of the flowers were touching the floor in front of it. It sort of looked like it was bowing. I thought maybe I had subdued it. Instead, it whipped its potted end and slammed it down against the side of the bed. The pot shattered into a number of pieces while the dirt around the roots kept its shape. The plant quickly picked up the largest pieces with its branches and began waving them in my direction. The clay pieces were jagged and sharp, and the way the plant was acting made me feel like I was in some sort of horticultural Western.

I just stood there in shock.

Freed from the weight of its pot, the plant sprang forward, hitting me in the stomach and slicing away at my hospital gown with its sharp, pottery shards. I tried to fight it off with my broken bottle, but it simply slammed three pieces of the cracked pot against my weapon and shattered it completely.

"Nurse Agatha!"

The plant was going at me like a tiger trying to claw its way into a bag of meat. I pushed it away and received three long scratches on my right arm. The wounds burned like fire and caused my body to react like a maniac. I kicked and screamed, my left foot punting the plant onto the bed. All the soil at the base of the plant exploded into the air. I could now see the plant's thin roots dangling like cooked ramen noodles. I scrambled up and tried to run again toward the door.

The plant leapt from the bed and wrapped itself around my legs.

I didn't know whether to scream, "Ahhhh," or "Agatha."

I went with, "Aaaaaagaaaathhhha!"

I wriggled forward on the floor, futilely clawing and grabbing at the slick tile. I could see the bell against the wall and above the desk. I suddenly wanted nothing more than to push it and have the entire staff run in and rescue me.

I kicked my legs in a desperate attempt to shake the plant off. All it did, however, was cause the plant to leap from my legs onto my back. I could feel the clay shards cutting through my gown and slicing my skin. I got onto my knees and tried to reach behind me and pull it off. As I reached out, the plant swung its noodlelike roots around and mashed them into my face. My eyes and nose were suddenly filled with dirt. I couldn't see clearly, and I could feel the plant now ripping up my shoulders.

It took everything I had to get to my feet and stumble toward the desk.

The plant pulled itself around my right side and began going at my face, its thorns digging in wherever they could. I fell to the desk and threw my hands against the wall searching for the call button. My left hand hit the button, and I pushed it. Even through the rain I could hear the muffled bell ringing somewhere down some faraway hall.

I pushed it again.

The flowers bit down on my hair and violently pulled my head backward. It felt like my neck was going to snap as I fell behind the desk.

"Heeeelll . . . !"

The smallest flower shoved itself into my mouth to silence me. I bit down and tore the bloom completely off.

The plant got angrier. It tore at me with a newfound aggression and anger. I felt a chunk of my hair being pulled out and the roots of the plant were frantically trying to wrap themselves around my neck.

"Helllp!"

Apparently nobody was coming. My whole body now burned from the deep slashes, and blood was dripping and smeared all over. I huddled under the desk as the plant continued to slice me up. I was just about to accept my fate when my elbow hit the large trash can under the desk. I tried to open my eyes to see if it was big enough to crawl into. I managed to get my left eye open enough to see that it wasn't just a trash can; it was an industrial-strength paper shredder.

My mind instantly came up with a plan.

I threw my head back against the top of the shredder, hitting the on button. The machine whirled to life as I grabbed the roots that were currently trying to strangle me. I yanked them back as hard as I could and shoved the plant's roots down over the long, thin opening of the shredder. Before the plant could react, I mashed the roots into the slot, hoping that at least one of them would catch.

It was better than that, the shredder got hold of a large wad of the noodly roots and quickly began to pull the rest of the plant in. The flowers and branches all dropped their clay pieces and began to writhe and wriggle in pain. The small, thin branches were frantically trying to grab hold of me to keep from being pulled in and shredded up. Some pulled my hair, and one of the flowers bit down on my left ear. But the machine was too powerful.

I pulled myself away and watched as the shredder chewed up all of the roots and began pulling in the base of the plant. The machine struggled for a few moments on the thickest parts of the plant but then got up to speed and sucked in the rest of it. The last part to be pulled in and ground up were the two remaining flowers. I think the biggest one was screaming. I tried to think of some cool comment to say, but all I could think of was, "Plant that."

I waited a few seconds to make sure it was really all finished, and then I reached over and turned the shredder off. I collapsed, lying down on the floor with my legs sticking out from under the desk. My entire body was cut up, and there was blood all over me and on the floor where I had dragged myself.

I slowly caught my breath wondering why nobody had come when I rang.

The doors pushed open. "What, what?" Nurse Agatha said stomping in. "There's no need to ring the bell more than once. I'm not a cow, you can just . . ."

She stopped talking and looked around. She gazed at my empty bed and then down at the floor. I watched her eyes follow the trail of blood to where I was.

I think it's kind of weird to hear old people swear.

I lifted my head up more and tried to smile as she ran up to me. I thought she was going to fuss and worry and attempt to help me. Instead she pulled my right arm up and yanked me into sitting position. She then stood up and pushed the call button four times.

Grown-ups are always contradicting themselves.

"Just what do you think you're doing?" she demanded.

"Bleeding," I answered honestly.

Two big male nurses burst through the door. They picked me up and carried me back over to my bed. As they were setting me down, Nurse Agatha was still carrying on.

"He's done it for attention," she ranted. "He's more trouble than a bus full of apes."

"It wasn't me," I said as one of the nurses began to wipe off my wounds and look me over. "It was the plant."

All three of them looked at each other.

"What plant?" Nurse Agatha asked.

"The one I thought you stole."

Now she really went off. I just closed my eyes and lay there in pain as they cleaned me up. It took almost two hours to get me bandaged and into clean clothes and sheets. In the end I had lost a couple of chunks of hair, had a nice-sized gash on my right leg, and hundreds of scratches varying in depth and length. According to Nurse Agatha I was "probably going to live."

They hooked my IV back up and gave me more medicine. The next couple of days were nothing but a blur.

Illustration from page 3 of The Grim Knot

CHAPTER 3

Really White Man

I CAN'T UNDERSTAND WHY people don't believe me, but for some reason nobody did. I tried to point out how stupid it would be for me to scrape myself up. But, as usual, not a single grown-up took the time to try and understand that. To make matters worse, I now had to stay an extra few days for observation. Of course, "observation" meant leaving me all alone in the large hospital hall. Someone brought me food three times a day and someone picked up my tray when I was finished, but that was about it.

There was one day when they brought a young kid in and put him in a bed three beds down from me. But the kid only stayed a few hours and he coughed the whole time so we never really had a meaningful conversation.

According to Nurse Agatha, Thomas had come by to visit

me, but I was sleeping and they had decided not to wake me up. I was pretty mad about that, seeing how I could have really used the company.

By my eleventh day in the hospital, I was so stir crazy I began having conversations with the squirrels that occasionally ran across the glass roof and played in the large pine trees that were surrounding the hospital.

I was way too bored.

I read one of the magazines Nurse Agatha had given me for the third time and tossed it down. The hospital didn't have any good magazines. I mean, me reading *Woman's World* once was embarrassing enough, reading it three times was just plain sad. Besides the lighting in the hospital wing was so bad it was hard to read. The glass ceiling let in almost no light, thanks to the thick gray clouds resting on it. I lay back in bed, sighed, and closed my eyes. When I opened them next, a man was sitting next to me on my right side. I screamed in a way that was unbecoming of any boy no matter how old he was.

The man put his right hand over my mouth as he held his left pointer finger up to his lips and shushed me.

"Quiet," he insisted. "They'll hear you."

That was the point. I thought I'd be happy to see anyone, but this man made me uneasy. The lack of light in the room made him look like a shadow. He removed his hand slowly and tried to smile. His smile reminded me of a cracker. As he turned up the sides of his mouth, dry bits of white, dry skin drifted off his old lips. He had on a brown robe with the hood hanging low over his head, covering the top of his eyes. I could only see the bottom of his green wire glasses. Despite the odd robe, the most obvious thing about this man was that he was white, and I mean *really, really* white. There was no mistaking him for anything but. His hands and chin were so pale they practically glowed in the low light.

"Who . . . ?"

He shushed me again.

"What's that smell?" I wasn't very obedient. I had been shushed, but I was still talking. I couldn't help it; the hall was suddenly filled with a bad odor. "Is that you?"

"That's not important," he insisted.

"I think it is," I said waving my hand in front of my nose.

"What happened to your face and arms?" he asked as if confused. "I checked in on you a few days ago and you weren't all cut up."

"I cut myself shaving."

Apparently, he believed that because he didn't question me further. He did talk, however. "Listen, I need your help," he said quietly, his pale cracker-looking lips crumbling even more.

"I don't . . ."

"Quiet," he snapped. "The stone—where is it?"

"What are you talking about?" I asked honestly.

The old man glanced around nervously. He looked up at the glass ceiling and then tilted his head as if listening to the soft rain that was falling. I wanted him to move so I could see him better, but he sat still. "You were there," he finally said.

"What?"

"You were there," he whispered. "When the last dragon vanished."

I nodded slowly.

"Where's the stone?"

"What?"

"Where's the stone?" he snapped while grabbing me by my hospital gown. "I need the stone."

"I don't know what you're talking about," I insisted.

"There had to be a stone," he rasped. "From the last dragon. Who's tending it?"

"It's gone," I said strongly.

"Gone?"

"I destroyed it."

His cracker mouth crumbled as he ground his teeth. "Don't lie to me. I must have that stone."

"I have no idea who you are," I said sitting up. "Nurse!"

My voice echoed down the long hall and was then drowned out by the gentle rain.

"Quiet," he growled. "Where's the stone?"

"I told you. I destroyed it. Who are you anyway?"

"That's not important."

"Nurse!"

"Quiet," he said, putting his hand back over my mouth and trying to sound a little more friendly. "I'm not here to hurt you."

I bit his hand letting him know that I was there to hurt him.

"Ooow," he cried, his hand snapping back. He jumped up and pulled a long sword from his side. "Do you think this is a joke? The soil will turn on you."

With the sword and the cape he looked a lot like a pale extra in a poorly funded fantasy film.

"What about the soil?" I asked, thinking back to the crazy plant and some of the things trees had been doing to me.

"It will . . ." he started to say.

I was kind of interested in what he was going to say next, but I didn't get a chance to find out because at that moment Thomas came through the doors at the end of the hall. He was holding a large brown paper bag and frowning. I looked back at the man with the sword and he was gone, but his smell was still there.

Thomas stepped down the hall and up to my bed. He set the paper bag on the end of my bed and smiled weakly.

"How's our little delinquent?"

I liked Thomas. He was stuffy and lovable. He always reminded me of someone who had traveled from the past and was now stuck here trying to fit in. He had thin shoulders and walked with a crooked gait. His nose was bulbous and jiggled like a water drop whenever he shook his head. He was usually wearing a felt cap and vest and sometimes had a cane that he didn't need, but which made him feel dignified. He currently had the cap and vest with him, but no cane.

"Did you see him?" I asked.

"See who?" Thomas questioned, looking around as if it were an assignment.

"There was a guy in a cloak—really white. Can't you smell him?"

Thomas sniffed the air in the most respectable manner and shrugged. He began to pull things out of the paper bag, not paying much attention to me. "It's hard to see anything too clearly here in this hall. I'm sure it was just one of the nurses. Now, I've brought you a few things to keep you entertained."

"Finally," I said with excitement.

He handed me a little tiny book that when you flipped the pages showed a stick figure wearing a top hat and jumping over a short fence. He had also brought a small chalkboard with a single white piece of chalk.

"Where do you shop?" I asked in disbelief.

Thomas just stared at me.

"Thanks," I smiled.

"Oh yes," Thomas added. "Wane thought you might want your dictionary." Thomas handed me my small yellow diction-ary. I had gotten it shortly after I had arrived in Kingsplot. I had wanted to look up the meaning of Wane's name. Since then I had been trying to slip cooler words into my vocabulary.

"I'm beholden to you," I said, using a word that actually wasn't that cool. "Do you have any idea when I can get out of here?"

"They want to keep you a few more days."

"I feel fine," I complained. "I need to get out."

"I think you'd better stay put," Thomas said. "There are many who think you should be locked up, seeing how you con-tinue to tear apart Kingsplot."

"It was an accident," I insisted. "I thought it was just a big ball."

"A ball? It was one of the old weather balloons," Thomas said. "In the olden days they used to float them up to experiment with the weather. I thought they were all gone. You should have just left it alone."

"I know."

"You're a magnet for mischief."

"I'm really sorry," I apologized.

"I'm certain you are," Thomas halfway smiled.

"So, aren't you going to ask me about all my scratches?"

"The hospital informed us about the details of your stunt."

"Stunt?"

"Although in all honesty," Thomas went on, "I'd say you were the last person who needed more attention."

"I didn't do anything for attention," I complained. "I was attacked by a plant."

"Yes, yes, the nurse told me," he said kindly. "Attacked by a plant, picked on by a shed."

"I never said the shed at Callowbrow was picking on me," I pointed out. "I just thought it was a big ball that we would be able to play with. Why won't anyone believe me?"

"That's enough," Thomas insisted. "Millie and Wane miss you."

"Yeah, I can tell by their constant visits."

"The manor keeps them busy."

"Of course. What about my dad?"

"He hasn't been down from the dome in quite a while," Thomas said sadly. "He was happy to hear you were okay."

"And Kate?"

"I don't know much about her business," Thomas said. "Millie did say she was hospitalized and released after a couple of days."

"And she hasn't come to visit me?"

Thomas patted me on the head, "The weather has been considerably wet."

"It's always wet," I complained.

"True enough," he said, trying to smile. "Wane will pick you up as soon as you're free to come home."

"Have you heard anything from Wyatt?" I asked.

"He's called a few times asking when you'll be home."

"When will I be home?"

"Hard to say."

Thomas patted me on the head again and left. I spent the rest of the afternoon with my flip book watching a little stick figure jump over a fence and worrying about Mr. Dry Mouth while wondering about the last stone. I wasn't completely sure that I hadn't just imagined the whole thing.

I was about to try to fall asleep when I got my third visitor of the day. The double doors swung open and a tall guy with a dark goatee and blue hoodie stepped into the hospital hall. He was thin, and his jeans were cuffed. He was displaying the type of smile you might see in a used-car salesmen's museum, and he was carrying a small stuffed animal.

I recognized him instantly and groaned.

His name was Van and he was a reporter for some newspaper far away. Ever since the pillage, he had been popping up in my life trying to get me to tell him more. He treated me like a little kid and spoke to me as if him saying the right thing might open me up and make me spill the beans. I hadn't seen him for some while.

"Beck," he said cheerfully. "How are you?"

"Fine," I answered, bothered.

"The correct answer is you're doing great," he said, grinning.

I hate it when people tell me how I am doing. "Why are you here?" I asked.

"Nice to see you too," he smiled. "I brought you something." He handed me the small stuffed koala. "I thought it might keep you company."

"Thanks," I said, embarrassed. "I can't wait to introduce him to all my other stuffed animals at home."

"His name is Binkers," Van informed me.

"Of course."

"Mr. Binkers," he added.

"I thought you had left Kingsplot," I said.

"I had, but then a friend of mine told me you had been causing more trouble, and I thought I'd come check it out."

"You came all the way back just for that?"

"Well, I had to see how my little buddy was doing."

I looked around wondering whom he was talking about. The last thing I was was Van's little buddy. He had written an article on my family that was far from flattering, and he was constantly trying to trick me into giving him more damaging information.

"Tell me, champ," he continued. "What happened?"

"I'm sure you've read the papers."

"I have, but there always seems to be more to you than the papers print," Van said.

"Well, if you think it had anything to do with dragons you're way off," I told him. "It was just me being careless."

"Dragons?" Van said in mock surprise. "I never said a thing about dragons, but now that you mention it . . ."

"That's so yesterday," I waved. "I'm sure most people have forgotten by now."

"Funny," Van said. "I still remember."

"Maybe you're special."

Van smiled. "The nurse said you cut yourself up."

I looked at the scratches on my arms. "Yeah, I fell."

"She said you told her a plant attacked you."

"Didn't she sign some sort of confidentiality thing to become a nurse? Why is she telling you anything about me?"

Van ignored my comment. "If my memory is correct, I think there were plants involved with the dragons."

"I can't remember," I said, not wanting to tell him a thing about the plant. "My memories are not as correct as yours."

"Oh, I think they are," he said slickly.

His face looked so dumb when he was trying to be smooth. He would sort of purse his lips together, making his chin look pointier and his goatee longer. His cheeks would push up toward his eyes, which rolled to the left just enough to make him look crazy.

"Listen, buddy," he whispered. "I'm not your enemy. I'm your friend. I just want to do your family justice. If we work together, we can make something positive out of this. Where'd you get the scratches?"

"I fell."

Van closed his eyes and breathed in through his nose. His eyelids sprang open and he stared directly at me. "You get some rest. We'll talk later."

"I'd rather not," I said nicely.

"Rest is important," he insisted.

I was going to tell him I had nothing against rest and that

what I meant was that I wasn't going to talk to him later, but I didn't want him hanging around any longer. He stood up and patted me on the head.

"I'm here for you," he said.

"I don't want you to be," I told him.

"You'll feel better with some rest," he said smiling.

He was telling me how I felt again.

"Enjoy Mr. Binkers," he added.

"As soon as you leave I'm going to hug him," I said.

Van turned, oblivious to the sarcasm. He walked down the hospital hall and out the double doors. I looked at the koala and wondered why Van couldn't have brought me a PSP or a laptop instead. I also wondered why most of my visitors were older people.

I fell asleep thinking about dragons, eucalyptus trees, and Kate.

Illustration from page 6 of The Grim Knot

CHAPTER 4

I'm Going Slightly Mad

THE NEXT DAY CAME AND WENT with no sign of anyone I really cared about. Nurse Agatha came in a couple of times, but she was little comfort seeing how all she did was berate me. She called me a ruffian the first time and a ne'er-do-well the second time. I kind of liked the odd words she used. I told her I liked her hat. She told me to hold my tongue. When I literally did as she asked, she pinched my cheek and called me a twit.

She looked at me until I was self-conscious and then sniffed, "Once a Pillage, always a Pillage."

"If you and I ever get married, I'll go by Agatha," I suggested.

"Disrespect," she snipped. "Your wit will burn you someday."

I wanted to tell her about all the times my wit had already burned me or caused me problems, but she walked off and left me alone again.

It had been almost six days since the plant had jumped me. A number of my scratches had healed leaving only the deeper ones visible. They too were beginning to fade. My brain was going numb from being kept locked up in the stupid hospital. Wyatt had called me once and we had talked on the phone for about an hour. I thought back to our first bad encounter and how he had turned into a great friend. He claimed he wanted to come visit me but that his parents would never bring him. When I reminded him that he had a driver's license and his own car, he confessed to being scared to death of hospitals and since I was going to live, he would just wait to visit me when I wasn't in one. I couldn't totally blame him. I wasn't that fond of hospitals either.

It rained all day again and just as afternoon was beginning to make an appearance, Wane entered the hospital hall pushing an empty wheelchair.

I was so happy I almost jumped out of my bed.

Wane's dark hair was really short, showing off her long, thin neck and small ears. She was smiling as if it were something she was supposed to do and not as if she were enjoying it.

She was pretty and one of the few adults I had ever met that I thought had any style.

"Ready to go home?" she asked.

"Yes," I said quickly. "I mean I'll miss all the activity here."

Wane looked around at the empty hall and tried to laugh. "You have to leave by wheelchair," she said. "'Insurance reasons.'"

"I don't mind being pushed around," I said, while throwing my legs over the side of my bed.

"I brought you some clothes," she said, handing me a bag. She turned around to give me some privacy. Inside the bag was a pair of jeans, a T-shirt, some unmentionables that I won't mention, a pair of shoes, and a silk vest.

"Let me guess," I guessed. "Thomas packed these clothes."

"Just hurry," was all she said.

As soon as I was dressed, Nurse Agatha came in and had Wane sign some papers. I told Agatha that I'd miss her, and she said something about youth being seen and not heard. Once she left, Wane just stood there staring off into the distance.

"Are you okay?" I asked.

"Fine," she replied with a sigh. "You're the one who's been hurt. Come on."

I plopped myself down in the wheelchair. Wane grabbed my pillow and the small bag someone had packed for me. She set them both in my lap, and without turning the wheelchair around, she began to pull me backward. I looked at the empty beds and the glass ceiling as I moved in reverse. I felt like I was traveling back in time, back to the moment before I had made the extremely poor decision to blow up the velvet balloon. My life was running in reverse. Wane said something, but it sounded warbled, like a record playing backward.

We moved through the double doors and Wane spun my wheelchair around. Like the wing I had been in, this area was empty and silent as well. Wane pushed me down a thin ramp and out two more wide double doors.

I could instantly feel the light rain on my face as we stepped outside. The smell was a fantastic mix of fresh dirt and water. The often-present mist of Kingsplot wrapped around me like a wet, but familiar friend. I felt like I had just been paroled from a life sentence.

Wane helped me into the car as if I were some unknown kid whom she was babysitting. She closed the door behind me and returned the wheelchair to the front desk. When she climbed back in, she didn't even look at me. She started up the car and pulled away from the hospital.

"You know, if I had my license, I could have driven myself home," I pointed out. I had been begging my dad to let me get my license, but something about the thought of me driving made him uncomfortable. He had told me to bring the subject up again in a few years.

Wane didn't reply.

"You're so quiet," I said.

"Nothing to say, I guess."

So we drove in silence. It had been almost a year since the dragons, and Kingsplot was busy and almost completely put back into place. And there were still a few places where construction could be seen. There were a couple of buildings on the edge of town that were not going to be rebuilt so they just sat there as new ruins.

"I bet Millie's mad," I said.

"Millie's fine," Wane snipped.

"Did I do something wrong?" I asked.

"Beck," Wane grumbled. "Do you even have to ask?"

"What?"

"You almost tore apart our town and now this."

"I didn't know the ball would explode."

"What did you think it would do?"

"I thought it was just a big ball," I said lamely. "We were going to roll it out and let everyone play with it."

Wane shook her head.

"I'm sorry." I couldn't wait to get home and visit Kate. She'd be nice to me.

"There's a limit," Wane sighed.

"You're not the one who usually gets mad at me," I pointed out.

"Well, I care about this place. And you," she tacked on.

We wound up and out of Kingsplot. The road grew thin and we threaded through dark tunnels as we climbed up the road. For the past few days all I could think about was getting back home. Now, however, I wasn't so sure. My dad, Aeron, was still adjusting to being a father, and even though he had been mostly kind to me, I knew he had a side to him that was a bit unsteady.

We passed a couple of the other large, tree-covered mansions and finally pulled in through the open gates and drove down the long winding driveway toward home. The huge mansion dwarfed any of the others around. It rose from the trees as we turned the bend, its seven stories pushing up into the wet, gray sky. Gargoyles leaned down at us from the roof, and fat, black clouds dotted the top floor, circling the copper dome where my father spent much of his time. I couldn't see his shadow up there, but then I didn't really have a great view of it. We drove through a stone archway and circled the large, twisted, snake-shaped fountain. Wane pulled up to the back door and stopped the car.

"Hop out," she said.

"You're not coming in?"

"I've got things to do."

"Is my father home?"

"I'm sure he's somewhere in there," she said ominously.

"I don't . . ."

"Hop out, Beck."

I got out of the car feeling like a jerk. My stomach and legs were heavy, and I felt guiltier than I had in a long time.

"It was just a balloon," I mumbled to myself as I shut the car door. "And a shed." Wane pulled away and I yelled after her, "It was just a shed!"

The serpent-shaped fountain gurgled and spit.

"Whatever," I said, brushing it all off.

I pulled open the back service door and walked into the one kitchen we actually used. Millie was there rolling out dough. She looked up, shook her head, and went back to rolling.

"You too?" I asked.

Millie tisked. She looked at me with her wrinkled, old face and opened her mouth as if to say something. Her mouth closed and she wiggled her head slowly. My stomach felt even worse. I liked Millie. She was like the grandmother I had never really had. She was less skinny than fat and one of her eyes didn't sit quite right. She was crotchety, but kind, and could cook better than anyone I had ever known. But now apparently she was giving me the silent treatment.

"I really am sorry," I pleaded. "I didn't think what happened would happen."

Millie grunted.

"I'm okay," I pointed out. "That's something, right?"

Millie sniffed. I could tell she wanted to be kind to me, but she was trying hard to appear tough.

"I feel so loved," I said.

"Beck," she scolded.

"It was an accident."

Millie shook her head.

I tried a different approach. "Thanks for the plant."

"It was the least I could do," she said.

I thought about telling her what her "least she could do" had done to me, but I let it go. I walked out of the kitchen and down the hall.

I climbed to the next floor, stepped across the large empty room to the larger stairs, and climbed up to my room. Everything looked almost the same as when I had last left it. My bed was still there, and it had been made up by someone. The windows were clean, but my old, unreliable, wind-up alarm clock was gone. Sitting in its place on my nightstand was a new battery-powered one.

I threw my things on my bed and turned around. I needed to talk to my dad. I walked quickly to the stairs and began the climb. My father had been spending some time down on the main floors, but he still spent most of his days up in the damaged copper dome that sat on top of the mansion. Our relationship was not like any father and son I had ever seen in a commercial or movie, but I loved him, and I think he loved me.

I reached the door leading into the dome and knocked. I could hear some shuffling, and then it was quiet. I knocked again, this time louder.

"What?" my father yelled in reply.

"It's me," I shouted.

"Come, come."

I pushed open the door, and a strong breeze from the open windows swirled around me. Some of the dome had been torn at by the dragons, and my father had done a poor job of repairing it. There was wood and wire sticking out of the walls and cracks in the floor. My father was in the center of the dome sitting in a stiff chair, leaning his head back. In his lap was a large book. His eyes were closed.

"I'm home," I said.

"That's stating the obvious," he said, without moving or opening his eyes.

"I'm fine," I said, bothered by his reaction. "In fact, I'm

great. That vacation was just what I needed. Oh wait, that's not completely true. I'm a little tired from all the kindness and well wishes everyone's been giving me."

"You're being funny, aren't you?" my father asked.

I growled lightly.

My father opened his eyes and moved his head to look at me. He was wearing a red silk robe with gray slippers and a long cap that made him look ridiculous. He had also shaved his beard.

"You seem to be attracted to trouble," he said.

"Yeah, she's really pretty," I replied.

"Your tongue is sharper than mine ever was."

I stuck my tongue out and tried to look at the tip of it.

"You could have killed yourself," he said. "And that young woman you associate with."

"Kate."

Aeron nodded. "Regardless, we're glad you're home."

"We?"

"The staff," he clarified. "And me, of course."

"Of course."

I don't know what my deal was, but I was ticked off. I know I messed up, but I had been in the hospital for over a week. The concern and caring from the few people I cared about was pathetic. Would it have killed my father to stand up and put his arm on my shoulder and tell me that he was glad I was home? Where was the "Welcome Back" pie that I had envisioned Millie making for me? Where was Thomas offering to help me up the stairs as if I were still in bad shape?

I looked out the windows and up toward the surrounding mountains. In the far distance, beyond the back gardens and past the conservatory where I had once grown dragons, I could see the long, wide field of stones. My mind flashed back to the visitor at the hospital.

"Some people stopped by," I informed him, "at the hospital."

"I would have come, but I've been busy," he said.

"I can see that," I answered, looking around. "One of the visitors was that reporter I told you about, Van. He came back to Kingsplot just to check up on me."

"People love to stare at deformity."

"I guess," I said confused. "The other visitor was an older man and he asked about the stone."

My father sat up straight.

"He thought I had it still," I added.

"Did he tell you his name?" my father asked cautiously.

"No," I answered. "But he was wearing a robe with orange circles on the sleeves and he was whiter than anyone I've ever seen. Plus he had a sword. I might . . ."

It's always kind of funny to see older people move fast. I mean, usually you just see teachers and parents going about their business at a normal speed. Occasionally you'll see some grown-ups jogging, and if you're unlucky you might experience the embarrassment of watching one of them dance, but for the most part, they just act like slow regular beings. So I found it rather humorous when my father jumped up out of his chair and began mumbling and shaking loudly. I made a mental note to always move slowly when I got older. My dad grabbed my shoulders. It wasn't quite the hug I had been expecting, but it was something.

"What are you doing?" I asked.

"That's not important. What else did he say?" my father demanded.

"Nothing," I insisted. "Like I said, he wanted the stone."

"Did you tell him where it was?"

"I said I destroyed it."

"Was there anything else about him you can remember?"

"I couldn't see him very well. But his lips were all cracked and flaky."

My father swore. He pushed me as he dropped his hands from my shoulders. Then he spun around, dropped to his knees, and began to rummage through some papers next to his chair and his wood trunk. I guess he found what he wanted because he yelped and stood up.

"Silly, huh?" I added.

My father stared intently at one of the papers in his hands. "Plays are silly," he said without looking at me. "This is serious."

"So who was . . . ?" I tried to ask.

"Are the stairs clear?" he snapped. He was always concerned about there being items blocking the stairs in our house. It was as if he imagined I got a thrill out of shoving couches and tables onto the stairs.

"The stairs are always clear."

My father twisted, grabbed his stick, and dashed out the door. The door slammed behind him, and I was alone in the dome.

"Welcome home," I sighed.

I returned to my room and lay down. My hope was that when I opened my eyes things would be less crazy.

It was a silly thought.

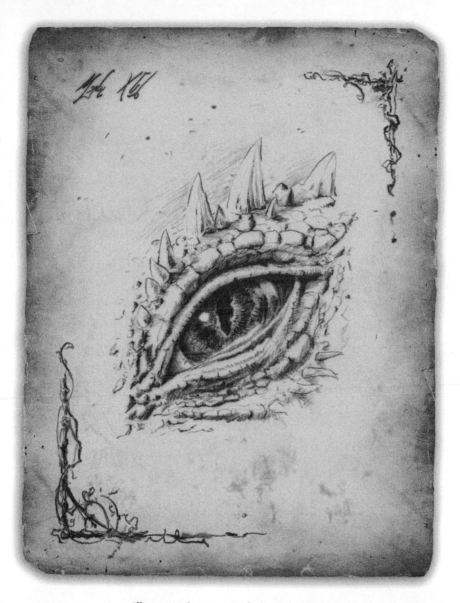

Illustration from page 7 of The Grim Knot

CHAPTER 5

It Is Late

I CAN'T REMEMBER FALLING ASLEEP, but I was pretty aware of waking up. Wind was working its way in through all the cracks and openings the huge old manor had. I tried to just close my eyes and go back to sleep, but I think my body was sick of being in bed. I sat up slowly and looked around in the darkness. The only light came from the red digital numbers on my new clock. The sound of something large creaking cracked through the air.

"Wane?" I whispered. "Thomas?"

There was no answer, only the slow whine of my bedroom door easing open. I scooted back in my bed and tried to see better in the dark. I could faintly see the outline of my opened door—there didn't seem to be anyone or anything standing in the doorway.

"Hello?"

Only the wind answered. I slipped out of bed and shuffled across the room and up against the wall. I reached for the light switch and flicked it up—nothing. I groaned; the power always seemed to be on the fritz. I moved to the open door and stuck my head out. The hallway was as dark as coal, and I could feel a stronger wind pushing through it like a slow train.

The wind picked up, and I could hear bits of dirt and debris tapping up against the windows as things blew around outside. A door banged open and shut somewhere down the hall.

"Just go to bed," I told myself. "It's only a door."

Apparently I wasn't in the mood to listen to myself because I had retrieved a small flashlight from my dresser, and I was now all the way out in the hall and slowly walking toward the banging door. Besides I was no longer tired at all.

I shined the flashlight down the long hall. I felt a little bit like I had when I had chased the light and discovered the basement. But unlike before, I knew the manor a lot better, and I figured there was nothing that could surprise me. I walked carefully down the hallway. The noise led me across the large open floor and over to where more rooms and doors were. The banging was getting louder.

"I'm coming," I said aloud.

I entered the far hallway that turned toward the south wing

of the mansion. I really didn't spend much time in that part of
the house. I mean the manor was massive and there were still a
number of rooms I had not investigated. I think I had ignored
the south wing because it didn't face the back gardens where
I had once been forbidden to look. So I figured it was just a
bunch of locked doors leading to empty rooms or stuffy old
bedrooms that were filled with prissy furniture covered in old
white sheets.

The wind was racing through the hall and I could hear the
door slamming much clearer now. I pointed the small glow of
the flashlight down the south wing.

After passing dozens of doors I came to the end of the
south wing hall. The last door on the end was opened. It
slammed shut and then popped open again from the surg-
ing wind. I pulled the door shut, and the wind bullied it open
again. I went into the room and could see that one of the windows was cracked open. I shoved it closed, and the wind began
to whistle in anger.

"Sorry," I said.

I left the room and closed the door behind me. This time
it stayed shut. As I turned to walk back down the hallway, the
beam of my flashlight washed over a small green door across
the hall. I moved the light back. The small green door looked
like a tiny cabinet or dumbwaiter entrance. I had seen other

unusual doors throughout the manor, but I couldn't remember seeing this.

I thought about just going back to my room and checking out the green door in the morning, but I was wide awake and I had a flashlight. The combination seemed perfect for exploring.

I knelt down and turned the knob. It was locked and there was no give. I ran my hand over the small green door and I could feel the dust collecting on my fingers. I smacked my palms together, and dust shot into my nose causing me to sneeze. When I lifted my arm to sneeze into my elbow, my hand knocked the top of the tiny door and my fingers snagged against the corner. I could feel something. I grabbed my flashlight and shined it on the top of the door. The trim was chipped and looked like it was coming off at the corner. I grabbed the corner with my free hand and pulled. The top popped away from the wall, and behind the back of the trim was a key wedged into the wood. I twisted the key free and held it up. It was brown and rusty and looked like an old house key. I didn't admire it for too long. Instead I shoved it into the lock on the small door.

It fit perfectly.

The door clicked open and immediately a belch of air blew out. The belch was followed by the wind from the hall racing in. I shined my light in but all I could see was more darkness.

I put the flashlight in my mouth and bent down to crawl in. I stood up and shined my light around.

I was kind of disappointed.

From what I could see it was just another room. There was a desk against one of the walls and a large mirror hanging near the right corner. I looked in the mirror and was surprised to see how scared I looked. Against the biggest wall there was an ornate fireplace with two cherub angels carved on the sides of it. The opening of the fireplace was almost big enough for me to stand up in. There was a regular-sized door near the mirror, but it was locked and boarded up. On the floor was a thick rug with a large woman wearing a crown stitched on it. On the sides of the rug there were a bunch of scarabs sewn around the edges.

It seemed like just another boring room, but the way the wind drew through the open door and howled across the room made me think that there had to be another opening some-where. I stood in the fireplace thinking the wind was just racing up the flue, but I couldn't feel any wind. I used my flashlight to carefully examine the rest of the fireplace. I had seen so many movies where there was a secret button or switch to open up a hidden door in the fireplace, so I just kept feeling around for anything that might work. I even reluctantly poked the cherubs' behinds thinking that just maybe their rears were the trigger.

They weren't.

As I was stepping around the side of the hearth, I could feel my foot hit something raised on the ground. I shined the light down and saw a small black tile that was slightly raised. I pressed my foot down and heard a click.

I looked around thinking the fireplace had opened up. It hadn't, but the mirror hanging near the corner was now glowing softly.

I turned off my flashlight.

The glow of the mirror was even stronger. I stood up and stepped over. The reflection on the mirror was gone and I could see a thin flight of stairs going up behind the glass. I reached out and grabbed the side of the mirror—it didn't budge. I took hold of the other side and it moved just a bit. I crammed my fingers around the edge and pulled. The mirror slid open like a glass door. The wind was flowing like a mighty river now.

"Whoa. I love this house."

The stairs behind the mirror were wooden and extremely narrow, barely wider than me. I stepped on the bottom stair and the wood creaked like a whistling monkey. The second step wasn't as bad. I turned around and slid the mirror closed. It snapped back into place with a soft click.

The mirror stopped glowing.

I flipped my flashlight back on and directed the beam upward. The passageway was only about three feet wide and the stairs appeared to go ten steps higher and then turn to the right behind a corner wall. There were cobwebs everywhere and it smelled like dusty glue.

I began to climb.

Wait, I heard myself telling me.

Thoughts began to slosh through my head like marbles being dropped down a waterslide. I thought about when I had found the basement and the sort of trouble it led to. I considered just going back to bed and pretending this was a dream. But I started to think about the look on my dad's face when I had told him about the visitor with the sword. I thought about dragons. I thought about the book, *The Grim Knot,* and wondered if there was any reference to weird mirrors in it. I thought about just once being responsible enough to ask permission to go exploring mysterious stairs before I actually did.

My thoughts settled at the bottom of my stomach, and, as usual, I ignored all the important ones and continued climbing.

I stopped to shiver and then resumed my climb. Dust popped off the stairs and into my light as I walked. There were cobwebs stretching across my path. Normally I'm not a big fan of cobwebs, but these cobwebs actually made me feel better. It was sort of a confirmation that this secret passage had not been used in sometime, which meant nobody besides me was around.

The stairs turned behind a wall and then ended. The passage was now long and level. I moved slowly, shining my light over every inch as I went. There was writing on the walls, but most of it looked like unreadable scribbles. There were a few words I could read. I saw the word "Time" and a large "Tell them."

Farther down the passageway was another mirror. I couldn't move it, but the beam from my flashlight went through it, letting me see the room behind. It looked like the room I had just been in, but there was no fireplace. I pushed up against the glass and could easily see every bit of the room.

I made a mental note: never change in front of mirrors anymore.

I turned from the mirror and continued down the passageway. After about twenty feet more there was a spiral staircase. The steps were so narrow that I had to turn sideways to climb up them. At the top there was another passageway that forked in two directions. I took the one on the left and accidentally stepped right through a huge spider web. I spent the next couple of minutes dancing around in a panic, trying to peel the webbing off.

Once I was relatively web-free, I kept moving. I was considering turning around before I got lost, when I reached the end of the skinny passageway and looked down. I appeared to be standing at the top of a wooden slide. I shined my flashlight, but the beam of light didn't reach far enough to see where the slide ended. It was narrow, steep, and tight, and looked like it raced down at least three floors.

I should have thought about it. I should have taken a moment to think things out. After all, that's what a rational, straight-thinking person would do. Instead I jumped down, held my arms up and slid.

Illustration from page 8 of The Grim Knot

CHAPTER 6

In Just Seven Days

I WAS MOVING SO FAST MY EYES couldn't keep up with my rapidly collapsing stomach. On most slides you simply climb up some stairs or steps, then slide down a metal or plastic surface, and arrive at a flat ending. Then you stand up, comment on how fast or slow you just went, and then do it again. The slide I was flying down, however, was nothing like that. This slide was made of wood and slicker than anything I had ever been on. I felt like a bar of wet soap slipping down a glass hill.

I tried to shine my flashlight in front of me but I was so busy flailing my arms that I couldn't get a clear glimpse of what was coming. The slide twisted and suddenly I was flying sideways and dropping fast.

The slide straightened out and then dipped, bouncing me up two feet and then slamming me back down. The passageway

was so tight, my shoulders kept hitting the walls as I raced.
I could see wood beams in front of me stretching across the
passageway. My head smacked the bottom of one. I threw my
body back and zipped under the rest of the wood beams. The
light from my flashlight flew back and forth like a spastic spot-
light.

I could see rats climbing on the wood beams. One fell from
above and smacked me in the face. I screamed and reacted
poorly by throwing my flashlight at it. It was a dumb move,
now I couldn't see anything.

The slide turned sharply again and I scraped against the
wall as I bounced around it. After two more dips and a short
spiral, it began to level out. My body slowed and I came to a
complete stop.

I lay there trying to catch my breath and patting myself all
over to feel if I was okay. It felt like my arms and legs were still
on, and I couldn't feel any bleeding. But I was covered in cobwebs that clung to my fingers as I tried to pull them off.

I had no idea where I was.

I sat up carefully. It was pretty obvious why nobody had
used the death slide in awhile. I scooted my legs off the side
of the slide and was happy to find solid ground. I eased myself
up and put my arms out in front of me to feel my way forward.

Within two steps I had reached a wall. I slid my hands along the cold stone surface feeling for any sort of light switch or door.

I could find neither.

I was about to bravely scream for help when the sound of a match being struck scratched behind me. Every hair on my neck stood up and froze. A soft glow filled the room and I spun quickly, throwing my hands up to protect myself from whatever it was. When nothing assaulted me, I slowly put my arms down and gazed at the light.

"You!"

The old, pale man with the sword was standing there holding a lit candle and staring right at me. The light glowing up into his shadowy face made him look like an ancient Boy Scout about to tell a ghost story. That wasn't really necessary, seeing how I was already completely spooked. We were standing in a narrow room with a brick floor and stone walls. I could see the end of the slide and there was a tiny table in the opposite corner behind the old man. I could also see a ladder on the wall.

"What are you doing here?" I asked nervously, stepping back.

Whitey hung his head and shook it slowly. He looked like someone who had just been caught doing something he shouldn't.

"I don't understand," I huffed. "Who are you?"

"There isn't time for questions," he insisted.

It was just like a grown-up to say something like that. In the time it had taken for him to say that he could have just answered my question.

"You must listen," he continued.

I nodded, slowly looking around for some way to escape.

"Where's that stone?" he asked.

"I thought you said there's no time for questions."

He moved one step closer and growled, "Listen, Beck, I am ill at ease."

"Maybe you need some sun," I offered kindly.

"I must know where that stone is."

"I destroyed it."

"That's a lie."

"Well, it's gone."

"Where?"

"I don't know."

"You don't understand."

"I really don't," I said honestly, trying to back up as far as I could.

"In seven days it will be too late and that stone will hatch, regardless of where you have put it."

"How . . . ?"

"Listen," he interrupted. "It will produce a queen. And you

must tend it or it'll be a perverted mess of a dragon with a mind of its own and no way to stop it."

"That's not true."

"Yes, I'm afraid it is," he said, his chin quivered in the candlelight. "You're the only one who can hatch it and destroy it."

"I don't believe you."

"You have the book," he insisted.

"*The Grim Knot?*"

He nodded.

"I've already read it," I informed him.

"I've heard there's more to it than words."

"I don't even . . ."

"Stop," he snapped. "You have started the ending by bringing those dragons to life, but now you have to finish it. You must plant it within seven days or she will destroy everything."

"She?"

"The queen," he growled impatiently. "Find the stone, nurture it as it grows, and then destroy her when she is born."

My mind was racing as fast as my body had been while falling down the slide. None of my thoughts made sense and I didn't know what to think. I didn't know who to believe. I had trusted Milo and he had turned out to be an old creepy magician. How did I know that this old man wasn't just someone weird in disguise? Maybe he was like the opposite of Milo. Instead of coming to me friendly-looking and turning ugly, he had started off ugly and mean but was going to turn friendly and then be nice to me.

Like I said, none of my thoughts made sense.

"In the hospital you said the dirt would turn on me," I reminded him.

"You have neglected your task. You're a Pillage. The soil's angry," he explained.

"Really?"

I couldn't see him clearly because of the way the candlelight was flickering, but I think he nodded.

"The stones must be stored properly or the soil will ruin them," he said hotly. "You didn't take care of the stone."

"I didn't know."

"How foolish your father has been."

I didn't like him talking about my father that way so I changed the subject. "I still don't understand why you're here. And what are these passages?"

"I was coming to see you," he insisted. "As for the passages, ask your father."

The old man pushed on the wall behind him. A part of the wall moved back and opened like a door. I could see and hear the outdoors. The old guy now looked nervous and shaky.

"So, you're a Pillage?" I asked, thinking he had to be related.

"Find the stone," he insisted, ignoring me. "Tend it properly and then destroy her when she is born."

"I can't find . . ."

"You must," he roared. "If not, in seven days it will be too late."

"Even if I could find the stone, where do I take care of it?" I argued. "Half of the conservatory is knocked down, and I've seen people hike through just to take a peek."

Whitey was silent.

"People are always trying to take pictures of the conservatory," I added. "There's not as many curious weirdos as there used to be, but I can't risk it."

"Interesting," he said. "Then look behind the garage."

"Where?"

"Behind the garage," he barked.

"Sorry," I said, taken back by his bark. "Do you know there's nothing but trees behind the garage?"

"Look down," he said nervously.

I looked at the floor.

"Not in here," he scolded. "Behind the garage. You'll find what you should follow."

"I . . ."

"You listen," he said hoarsely. "I'm taking a great risk

coming here, but you're taking a far greater risk abandoning that stone."

"My father's said nothing about stones growing by themselves."

"Your father knows nothing of dragons," Whitey said. "He has chosen to hide himself instead of participate. His ignorance is self-inflicted and may be the ruin of us all."

"Don't . . ."

He interrupted me again. "You have seven days."

"Okay, okay. Starting now?" I asked. "And does that mean exactly seven days, or is it sort of an estimate?"

"This is no joke," he insisted. "Seven days."

I was going to say more, but the old man pinched out the flame on the candle and slipped out the open wall. It was dark, but the moonlight outdoors was spilling in, making it possible to see the outline of things. I could hear the sound of falling water. I stepped though the door and was surprised to find myself in the courtyard near the twisted snake statue. I looked at the wall I had just come through and carefully pushed it closed. Once it was shut it was impossible to tell it was there. The patterns of the stone hid any trace. I looked across the courtyard to where the back door was and marveled over this secret place being there all along.

"Who designed this place?" I whispered.

I looked up at the gargoyles hanging off the top floor, but they didn't answer me. I walked over to the back door and made my way up to my father's room. I had a few things that I needed to ask him.

When I got to the top floor and knocked on his door, there was no answer. I knocked louder but there was still no reply. I pushed the door open and stepped into the room. The windows were open, and a soft wind was blowing around. The light switch didn't work but I could see the outline of the few pieces of furniture.

"Dad," I called.

No reply.

"Dad."

I was alone. I climbed down the stairs to the floor below but there was still no sign of my dad. I sat down in a large wingback chair to wait for my father to come back. I was a little worried, but more than that, I was a lot intrigued.

Illustration from page 9 of The Grim Knot

CHAPTER 7

Don't Lose Your Head

I WAS HAVING A VISION ABOUT finally getting a cell phone when the sound of bells began ringing in my head. My mind tried to focus on the noise, but I couldn't make sense of it. I shifted in the chair, and my butt slid forward, causing my whole body to slip out of the wingback and fall to the floor. The right side of my head smacked the wood floor, and a new kind of ringing bounced between my ears and behind my eyes.

I blinked and moaned simultaneously.

The original ringing grew louder and more obnoxious. I rolled over and pushed myself up. I now recognized the sound of the bells Millie and Wane used to summon people in the manor. The home was so massive that there was a system of bells to call certain people. The bells were located all over the manor, and they were activated in the kitchen. There were probably thirty of them. One bell rang the other kitchen, one rang the dome at the top of the house, one rang Thomas, one rang Wane, one rang the main library, one rang the banquet hall, one rang my room, etc, etc. . . . Whenever I didn't respond to the one in my room Millie would ring all the bells hoping I would hear at least one of them.

"I'm coming!" I yelled, knowing she couldn't hear me.

The bells kept ringing as I stood up and tried to get my wits about me.

"I'm coming! Stop ringing those stupid bells!"

They didn't stop. I climbed down all the floors and finally made it to the kitchen. Millie was there pulling the bell strings as quickly as she could.

"I'm here!" I yelled.

She stopped pulling and turned to look at me. Her expression was not friendly.

"Where were you?" she demanded.

"Sleeping."

"I rang your room."

"I wasn't there," I pointed out. "I went to talk to my father last night but he wasn't there. I guess I fell asleep in a chair waiting for him."

"He's not here," she said.

I wondered if anyone ever really heard me. "I know."

"He's gone," she said in a huff.

"I know," I said again.

"There's a note," Millie said, sounding like someone who had just found a new mole on their nose. She handed me a yellow piece of paper that was ripped along the top edge. There were only ten words. "I have gone after something important. Keep Beck here! Aeron." I read the ten words and looked at Millie.

"He never was very wordy," she said in his defense. "And he never leaves the manor. He went out last year when the beasts were pillaging, but he's been here ever since."

Millie talked about the pillaging as if it were a school social.

"So you think he's here in the manor somewhere?" I asked.

"No."

I loved Millie, but she was a way better cook than conversationalist.

"When I talked to him yesterday he actually ran out of the room," I told her. "He was kind of acting aberrant."

Millie stared at me. "Are you still reading that dictionary?"

I nodded.

"Well, what did he say right before he left?" she questioned.

"He said 'I'm going to write a brief note to confuse Millie. But I'll really just be in the bathroom.'"

Millie stared at me with her one straight eye.

"Sorry," I said staring at her with my two brown eyes. "So where are Thomas and Wane?"

"They've gone into Kingsplot."

I desperately wanted to tell Millie about the pasty man I had spoken with in the secret room right behind the kitchen, but I knew it would only make things more confusing for her. Besides, I didn't want to talk to anyone but my father about the man until I had checked out the area behind the garage.

"How about I start looking for my dad," I suggested.

"Have some breakfast first," she insisted. "It's not much, but I've made some toast and eggs and a few sausages. And some bacon and flapjacks with warm syrup."

"No orange juice?" I joked.

"I just squeezed some," she said glumly.

"It'll be okay," I told her naively. I was actually happier that Millie was now speaking to me than I was worried about my father. He was sort of different, but I knew he was capable of taking care of himself. "He would never be away from your cooking for too long."

"There's a good soul down in you," Millie smiled. "It's always a treat when it surfaces."

I smiled the way she liked me to and started into the breakfast. The orange juice and flapjacks were amazing.

After finishing off more than my share, I called Wyatt to

invite him up, but he wasn't home. So I ran outdoors and across the property to the garage.

The garage house was immense. The garage was long enough to park ten cars and deep enough to add thirty more. It was made of stone and the roof had several chimneys and dormers. There was also a huge weathervane on top of a tall stone cupola. The weather vane was in the shape of a cherub, but lightning had struck it so many times that it was burnt and the head had been blasted off. Now it looked like a charred, headless baby. There were storage rooms and offices on both sides of the garage as well as an upper floor filled with more rooms and mounds of junk. The stables were right next to the garage house, and they were almost as large but relatively empty at the moment.

I walked up the driveway and around the side of the garage. The area behind was heavily forested with thick pines and thin white trees. There were some doors and windows on the back of the garage, but most of them were rusted and looked as if they had not been opened or fiddled with for quite some time.

I put my hands on my head and looked around. I had no idea what I was searching for, and all I could see was forest. I did what Whitey had told me to, but there was nothing to see on the ground but dirt and leaves and an occasional bit of stone. I was kind of surprised not to find Old Whitey out there practicing with his sword.

"This is stupid," I told myself. "I'm going to see Kate."

I returned to the manor, took a shower, and changed into a black T-shirt and jeans. I was excited to go see Kate. I figured she was mad at me for almost killing her and that was why I hadn't heard anything from her. My hope was that once I smiled at her and said something charming, she would forget my mistakes and forgive me.

I jogged down the stairs and burst out of the back doors on the opposite side of the main kitchen. It wasn't raining, but there was plenty of mist to give you that overall feeling of moistness.

I took the brick driveway to the far edge of the house.

"Beck," a voice startled me.

I turned, and there was Van taking pictures of the manor. He was still wearing the same blue hoodie, and his dark goatee and hair looked disheveled.

"What are you doing here?" I asked, quite annoyed. "You're not allowed on our property."

"Calm down, sport," he said, holding up his arm and showing me his left palm. "I told you we'd talk later, and I just wanted to make sure you made it home all right."

"I'm fine," I said. "Now leave."

"How's Mr. Binkers?"

"I threw him away," I lied. There was no way that I was going to give him the satisfaction of knowing that at this very moment Mr. Binkers was sitting on my dresser looking out the window.

"I'm sorry to hear that," Van said, sounding as if I had just informed him that my best friend had died.

"You can go now," I said pointing down the driveway.

"I want to help you, Beck," he pleaded with mock compassion. "If there's something bothering you I can help."

"Okay," I agreed. "There's this reporter that won't leave me alone. Can you help me throw him off my property?"

Van laughed, which only made me like him less.

"Seriously," I added.

"Listen, Beck, you don't want me off your property," he said as if he was a hypnotist and he was trying to put me into a trance.

"Stop telling me what I want or how to feel," I insisted.

"Fine, but you need to understand, I'm cool to you because I like you. But what you did with those dragons was no joke. It's unbelievable, and the world deserves to know more. Plus, you tore up a town," he informed me needlessly. "I'm not the enemy; I'm here to help you, champ. I just want to see you and

Kingsplot safe. And I want to know what you know. You need me, Beck."

Now it was my turn to laugh.

"Tell me what happened," he demanded, his tone suddenly harsh. "Are there more dragons?"

"Dragons aren't real," I told him.

I could tell by his trembling hands that he would have liked nothing more than to reach out and grab me, but he took a moment to cool down. "Beck, just what are you up to?"

"I don't have to tell you anything," I said, backing away. "Now go."

Van closed his eyes and pinched the bridge of his nose with his left hand. When his eyelids opened, he took in a deep breath and smiled. I could see that his teeth were discolored.

"How about I come back later?"

"No thanks," I told him.

"All right," he winked. "I'll catch you later."

He turned around and started walking down the driveway. He looked back once, and I waved.

"Bye," I hollered nicely.

I waited until I could no longer see him and then left the driveway and entered the gardens heading toward Kate's house. I ran halfway across the back gardens, jogged until I reached the partially destroyed conservatory, and then walked quickly the rest of the way. I lost some time when I tripped over a tree root I had not seen and banged up my shin. In total it took about twenty minutes before I saw any sign of Kate's place.

Kate's family lived in a large cabin. It had once belonged to my family, but they had sold it to her family years ago. According to Kate, there was some trouble with the sale and since then her parents had not exactly been warm to my family. I had seen her mom and dad a number of times and I could tell that it took everything they had in them to even acknowledge me. I tried to warm them up with my wit and smile, but that always seemed to make things worse.

Kate's house had a large wooden front door with a metal goat's head hanging on it. Dangling from the goat's mouth was a big metal ring that, if swung properly, made a terrific thumping noise on their door. I knew they used the side door more often, but I liked using the knocker so much I always went through the front.

I pounded four times and then stood there like a delivery boy with no goods.

After a few minutes the door swung open and there was Kate's mother. Kate's mom was pretty with dark brown hair and a round face. She was thin and always wore shirts with flowers stitched on them. I smiled and waved at her. She didn't wave back.

"Is Kate home?" I asked.

"You dare?" she bit.

"I do?"

"You almost killed our daughter."

"I was hoping to apologize," I explained.

"Apologize? Apologize?"

I wasn't sure why she said it twice, but I nodded as if her response was extra good.

"Actions speak louder than words," she snapped.

That just confused me, so I sort of did made-up sign language with my hands as I asked, "Can I speak with Kate?"

"You may not."

"But Mrs. Figgins, I . . ."

"Don't Mrs. Figgins me," she demanded.

"Okay, Laura, then," I said trying her first name instead. "I just . . ."

I know it's not really possible, but I think I saw steam coming out of her ears. I wasn't trying to make her angry, but my personality was doing me in. I decided to stop talking.

"If my husband knew you were here, he'd box your ears," she raged. "You have been nothing but trouble since the moment you came to town. Now get off our property. The same property your family once tried to cheat us out of."

She pointed down their driveway and I followed her finger

with my gaze. I then looked back to her. I would have tried to say something polite, but my mind was preoccupied with wondering what "box your ears" meant.

Kate's mom slammed the door.

I stood there for a few seconds and then turned and started down the gravel driveway. I felt bad all of a sudden, and my stomach hurt as a good bit of guilt settled over me. I know I'm not exactly the best kid. I've tried at times to at least be acceptable, but it doesn't come easy for me. I've heard people talk. Some say that it's my confusing upbringing, or that I'm a victim of my environment. But deep down I know it's really just me. I keep hoping that I'll grow up to be something respectable, but even I wouldn't bet on that. The last thing I wanted to do was hurt Kate or make her parents mad, but for some reason everything I did seemed to work toward that end. I kept telling myself that I was going to change, but at the end of the day I usually just made things stickier.

"Not this time," I said aloud to myself. "This time is going to be different."

I would have been more convincing if, while I was thinking about going straight, I hadn't turned around, walked through the woods, and circled back around Kate's house and over to the bushes behind her window. I had a palm filled with small rocks that I was planning to throw to get her attention.

Like I said, don't bet on me changing too quickly.

I threw one of the small pebbles at Kate's second-story window. It tinked off the glass and dropped back down onto the ground. I threw two more and they too fell down without a response. I was looking around, contemplating on throwing something bigger when I heard the window open. I glanced up and there she was. Kate was beautiful, some of her red hair was loose in front of her right eye and she had on a blue T-shirt that said "Irish" across the front. There was a smile on her face, but the smile was quickly replaced by a frown.

"Beck," she said in a hushed tone. "What are you doing here?"

There were a million things I should have said to her, but I went with, "What does 'box your ears' mean?"

"What?" she asked confused.

"Your mom said your dad would box my ears."

"She's just saying that," Kate told me. "It means he'll knock your block off."

"My block?"

"Your head."

"Well, that's not very nice."

"Beck, is that really why you came to my window?"

"No," I said, angry with myself for being unable to have a normal conversation. "I came to see if you're okay."

"I'm fine," she said, looking from side to side. "But I'm not supposed to talk to you."

"I know."

"You look pretty scratched up," she said compassionately. "Are all those scratches from the balloon?"

"No," I answered, staring at my arms. The cuts the vicious flowers had given me had actually healed pretty well. Most of them were kind of hard to see now. "And for the record, I really did think it was a ball we were blowing up. These scratches are from a plant. But that's not important. I found something."

"A plant?"

"It's a long story," I waved. "But I found something."

"What?" she asked, sounding irritated. "You find a lot of things."

"This is different," I said defensively. "I found a secret passage in the manor. And there was a man."

"A secret passage?"

I nodded.

"And you found a man?" she added.

"Kinda. Actually I sort of ran into him. He . . ." I was sick of talking up to her window. "Can't you come out?"

Kate looked from side to side and then behind her. She focused her gaze back down toward me. "I do need to deliver eggs."

Kate's family had two huge chicken coops and their chickens produced a lot of eggs. They sold them to locals and a couple of small farmers' markets in Kingsplot. It was Kate's job to deliver the eggs to those houses that were not too far from her home.

"So, can you deliver eggs now?" I asked excitedly. "I know Millie ordered some."

"I'm not sure my dad has them ready."

"Well, as soon as you can, will you meet me behind my garage?"

"It might be an hour, Beck."

"Just hurry as fast as possible. I found a secret passage," I reminded her.

Kate looked around nervously. "Okay, I'll be there."

"That's what I like about you," I said, smiling.

"You like everything about me," she reminded me.

She had a good point. Kate closed her window, and I shrank back into the bushes. I was going to just walk home, but I heard Kate's dad talking loudly to someone on the other side of their house—so I ran a little. I had no desire to lose my head and end up looking like the weather vane on top of the garage house.

Illustration from page 11 of The Grim Knot

CHAPTER 8

Good Company

I STOOD BEHIND THE GARAGE for almost half an hour. I became so bored I started to collect pinecones and throw them at things. It was more fun than just standing there, but still nothing great. After the wind blew one of the pinecones back into my face, I decided to do something different. So, I began to climb some of the trees the pinecones had fallen from. The trees had no low branches, making it hard to get started. But I found two trees that were close enough together that I could inch my way up with my hands and feet on one tree and my backside against another. I reached a low branch and pulled myself up to sit on the limb. As I was grabbing the next branch the one I was sitting on snapped. I fell to the ground landing on a bunch of long-dead leaves and soil.

I believe the expression is "Ooooof."

I stood up and dusted myself off while wondering why I was having such a rough time with trees lately. It seemed as though wherever I went the trees and bushes were reaching out to mess with me.

I stared up at the back of the garage, wondering if it could possibly be any more boring. The stone seemed particularly gray and bland. I was wondering why they never built houses out of colored marbles or actual Legos when Scott, the groundskeeper, came around from between the garage and stables.

He saw me and nodded.

Scott was older than Wane, but younger than Thomas. He had deep, dark eyes and was usually wearing work gloves and a knit cap. He and I sort of got along. It had been him that had tried hardest to keep me away from the conservatory. And it had been his lack of success at doing so which led to me growing dragons and wreaking havoc on Kingsplot. Yes, most of the town blamed me, but I secretly blamed Scott.

"What are you up to?" he asked suspiciously.

"I was trying to climb that tree." I pointed to the tree that had dropped me. "But I fell. Now I'm bored."

"You're welcome to help me prune the ivy by the front gate."

I stared at Scott. "I'm not that bored."

He shook his head. "Youth."

I shook mine and smiled. "Gardeners."

Scott walked off to leave me alone with myself once more. I found a stick, drew a picture of a car in the dirt, and then brushed it away with my feet. I tried to see how high I could jump by stretching my arms above my head and springing straight up.

"Are you okay?" Kate asked from behind me.

I turned around quickly, embarrassed at being caught jumping. "I thought I saw a fly."

"Sure," she smiled.

Kate had on her same T-shirt and faded jeans. She looked like someone who was too pretty and cool to hang out with me. I wasn't sure what to do. I mean I had almost killed her, and I didn't understand enough about crushes to know the proper gesture to make after doing something like that.

"I'm glad you're okay," I said.

"Me too," she replied.

"I bet you're pretty happy that I'm okay," I added, trying to help her.

Kate smiled and then took my hand. I guess her mom was right; actions really do speak louder than words.

I told Kate all about the plant that had attacked me and the pale person who had come to visit me in the hospital. I filled her in on the mirror I could open and how some slides are way better than others. I then told her everything about Whitey breaking into the manor and how he had told me about the stone and looking down behind the garage and how according to him we only had seven days. I also told her how I had searched, but there appeared to be nothing here.

"He wants you to grow that last stone?" Kate asked in disbelief. "Is he aware of what the other dragons did?"

"I don't think he gets out much."

"You can't even find the stone, can you?"

"I've never really tried," I said. "I've thought about it a lot, but last time I messed with those stones, things didn't turn out so great."

"What's behind this garage anyway?" Kate asked, looking around.

"Nothing," I answered her.

"Well, if he's wrong about the garage, maybe he's wrong about everything." Kate looked up at the back of the building. She walked along the entire wall glancing up and down. She studied each window and door and inspected the trees right behind it. She ended her investigation by staring down at the dirt. "Maybe if we got up on top we could see something. He said look down, right?"

I thought it was kind of a dumb idea, but I had never been

on top of a garage, and the idea seemed rather appealing. Maybe I could find the burnt cherub head.

"Come on," I waved. "We can go up and out of those dormers."

We ran to the side and went through one of the doors. There were tools hanging all over as well as oil and dirt stains on the floor. The room was large. We walked across it and through a tall skinny door. That door opened up into a short hallway with stairs at one end. We climbed up the wooden stairs and into a room filled with tons of old junk.

"What is all this stuff?" Kate asked.

"Who knows?" I replied. "Maybe this is where Thomas shops. There!" I pointed to a metal spiral staircase in the corner.

The stairs led to an attic that was filled with boxes and smelled like dryer lint. I could see one of the back dormer windows. Kate followed me through the boxes to the window. It took me pushing and Kate cranking the window handle for us to get it open.

The outside world drifted in, smelling much better than lint. We stuck our heads out and looked down.

"See anything?" I asked.

"The trees are too tall."

Kate was right, the trees were almost right up against the

window, making it impossible to get a wide view. I grabbed onto the window frame and put my right leg out. I twisted and pulled my other leg while hanging onto the rock dormer and climbed outside. The roof was slanted beneath the window, but just above the dormer it was flat. I sat down on the slanted roof and reached back.

"Here," I said to Kate. "Give me your hand."

I helped pull Kate out and we crawled carefully to the flat roof.

"If we go over there we can probably see best," she said, pointing to the cupola that had the weather vane on top.

We walked along the flat ridge of the roof and up to the cupola. The cupola shot up out of the roof about ten feet. It was probably six feet wide and there was a large arch-shaped vent with wooden slats on all four sides. I was surprised how big it really was. From down below it had looked like nothing great, but now standing beside it, I was pretty impressed. The top of the cupola was a triangular roof, and on top of that was the weather vane. I walked up to it and looked through one of the vents.

"What's in there?" Kate asked me.

"I can't really see."

We both pushed our eyes up to the slats and stared through. It was black inside and just as my eyes were focusing, a big chunk of the blackness moved. Kate screamed as something burst through the vents. I flew backward grabbing Kate's shoulder and pulling her down as hundreds of black birds burst out of the vents. The birds screeched and flew upward. I slid down the slate tiles and slammed into one of the brick chimneys. I tried to get my bearings but the birds swirling around me made my head spin.

"Kate!"

"Over here!" she yelled.

Kate was hanging onto the edge of the flat ridge. Her feet were scrambling as she tried to get back up. I turned my body around and crawled up to meet her. The birds began to break up and settle back into the vents and cupola. I sat down on the ridge next to Kate and watched the last of the birds disappear.

"Why'd you scream?" Kate asked.

"That was me?" I asked in surprise. "I thought it was you."

Kate put her head in her hands.

"I don't really like birds," I admitted.

"Yeah, me neither," she said.

We sat there catching our breath looking out over the forest toward the mountains behind the garage house. The tall trees blocked most of our view, but there was a section where they were all shorter and thinner so we could see over the top of them. It looked like a fuzzy road leading up to the high, for-ested mountain.

We moved to the edge of the roof and looked down. There was nothing but the little bit of dirt before the trees started.

"See anything?" I asked.

"Looks just like it did when we were down there."

As we were working our way back to the dormer window a thought struck me. I stopped and gazed back out at the trees.

"Hey, is that one section of trees shorter?" I asked.

"Trees grow different heights," Kate pointed out.

"No," I insisted. "Those are all shorter, leading up to the side of the mountain. It's like only those were cut down and replanted years ago."

Kate looked closely at the forest.

"There's a long swath of short trees," I insisted.

"Swath? Are you still reading that dictionary?"

"I have it in the bathroom," I said.

"Nice," Kate smiled. "It is kind of odd how only those trees are short. Maybe someone cut them down for wood."

"Just that long strip?" I asked. "Why not cut down a square of them, or a rectangle, or just pick one here and one there?"

We climbed down through the dormer and out of the ga-rage. We got back outside and walked up to where the line of short trees met up with the rear of the garage. We both looked up and down a few times and then stared at each other.

"That old man was just crazy," Kate said. "There's nothing behind this place."

I walked slowly, looking carefully at the base. I think I was hoping that just maybe there was a buried basement like the manor had—there wasn't. But due to the lighting at the moment I did notice something small and rusty showing at the base of the back wall directly in front of the line of short trees. I thought it was just a small chunk of iron, but I couldn't pull it out.

"So what is it?" Kate asked, kneeling down, trying to dig at it with her hands. "Get a shovel or something."

I called Kate bossy, then ran into the garage and found a hoe and a shovel. I brought them both out and handed the hoe to Kate. She stood up and I lifted my shovel and threw the tip of it down into the dirt. I thought it would slice into the soil and I'd be able to dig up under and pop the metal piece out. Instead, my shovel head hit something metal and jammed my arms. The sharp, clinking noise pierced my ears.

"Ouch," Kate said, holding hers.

A chunk of dark dirt cracked open and we could see that the small piece of metal was at least ten inches long. We both stared at it.

"You know what it looks like," I said. "Part of a train track."

We both gazed back toward the long stretch of shorter trees. Kate dropped to her knees and began to search near the edge of the garage for the other side of the track as I dug at mine.

"Here's something," she said excitedly.

I stepped over and dug at it with the shovel. I could see a few inches of the other train rail. The rails were buried about two inches under the soil and appeared to run right into the back of the garage.

"Hold on," I said, dropping the shovel. I ran back into the side door we had entered before. I wanted to see if the tracks came under the wall and inside. I walked through the first room past the stairs we had climbed up. There was another door and when I walked through it there was a wide room with rows and rows of shelves on the walls. The back wall was extended into the room and was slanted.

Kate was standing by me now.

"I wanted to see where the tracks led," I explained. I walked around the large, slanted wall looking for a door or opening to get into what had to be a large space behind it. There was no opening. In fact it looked a little like someone was trying to hide the odd wall with all of the shelving. "The tracks must angle down lower because of the slant. So whatever was on those tracks would just disappear down beneath the garage. But someone sealed off the tunnel."

"Nice work, Nancy," Kate said. "Scooby and the gang would be proud."

I ignored her. "But why?"

"Who knows what your ancestors were thinking," Kate said. "They were nuts. Maybe the tracks lead to the buried basement."

We went back outside to where the small pieces of exposed rails were. I felt the back wall as if I were psychic and it could tell me something. It didn't say a word. It was just a cold, stone wall.

"Well, we can't knock down the wall," Kate said.

"But we could follow the tracks into the forest," I smiled. "I mean we could see where the other end is."

Kate looked to the trees and then back.

"Sorry, but I have to get home," she said reluctantly. "My parents will be wondering where I am soon."

"How about tonight?" I asked. "I have that metal detector that Millie bought me. "We could use that to track the rails. I'll get Wyatt up here too."

"You're already in trouble," Kate pointed out. "Remember?"

"Maybe this will help make things right," I suggested.

"Right," Kate smiled. "I can tell you're only interested because it might help."

"Mysterious train tracks leading into a forest," I argued. "How am I supposed to leave that alone?"

"Okay, I'll meet you at midnight," she gave in. "And I want to see that secret room and slide."

"Of course."

We quickly covered up the little bit of track we had found and went our separate ways.

Midnight couldn't come soon enough.

Illustration from page 18 of The Grim Knot

CHAPTER 9

Blurred Vision

I WAS SO EXCITED I COULD barely contain myself. To be honest, I had been a little bored the last few months and the thought of something weird and mysterious made things better. Sure, the balloon incident had broken things up, but I missed the drama the manor and dragons had originally provided my life. Things had gotten sort of normal and I was happy with the possibility of adventure.

I telephoned Wyatt and filled him in. Most of his questions had to do with the train tracks. "Yes, there are tracks," I insisted.

"And they lead into your garage?" he asked.

"They lead to the back wall and inside there's a large part of the garage no one can get to where the tracks go down."

"Who built that place?"

"I'm wondering about that myself," I said. "So can you make it?"

"I wouldn't miss it for the girls."

Don't get me wrong, I liked Wyatt. He was rough, but funny. Originally we were enemies, but the dragons had made us friends. The only thing that bugged me about him was the way he always joked about girls. He said things like, "Girls rule and I drool." He also liked to brag about how he was going to ask a bunch of them out. So far he hadn't asked anyone out. All he did was drive Kate and me crazy with his wishful thinking and desperation.

"So you'll be there?" I questioned, adding a fake laugh.

"Do girls like me?" he said confidently.

"No," I answered.

Now it was his turn to fake laugh. "I'll be there."

The rest of the afternoon dragged, and at dinnertime there was still no sign of my dad. There was, however, roast beef, fluffy mashed potatoes, dark gravy, sweet corn, and pie that was tastier than any pie I had ever eaten. As usual I ate at the counter in the kitchen by myself while Millie puttered around me cleaning up.

"You should sell this recipe," I said honestly.

Millie smiled for the first time since I had been home.

"You're a nice child, Beck. I just wish your father would show up."

"He said he was going after something important," I reminded her. "That's gotta take at least a day."

"I suppose," she said sighing and drying her hands on her apron.

"Millie?" I asked. "What do you think about trains?"

"I haven't given it much thought, but I suppose I like them. Why?"

I just shrugged. I guess I was hoping she knew and would suddenly blurt out the answer to where those tracks went.

"It was windy last night," Millie said.

"I know. Plus I'm having kind of a hard time sleeping," I told her. "I think it's because of all that time in the hospital. I'm sorry if my wandering around wakes anyone up."

"I didn't hear you wandering," she insisted.

"Last night I actually walked outside for a little bit," I told her. Just to stretch my legs."

"The outdoors can be quite invigorating," she replied.

I sighed, feeling better about having to slip out later and follow the tracks. After all, I would just be stretching my legs again.

After dinner I went straight to my room. I lay in bed and looked at *The Grim Knot* for about an hour. I reread some of the pages and stared at all the notes and pictures that were drawn in it. I knew there was more there somewhere. I just couldn't see it. The book was kind of like the manor, filled with secrets and hidden things you couldn't easily distinguish. I wished my dad was around to talk to, but chances were even if he were here he wouldn't say much about the book. It wasn't a subject he enjoyed talking about. I stared at one of the pages as if it had some hidden picture that would pop out at me. My new pasty friend had told me to look closely, but I couldn't see anything I hadn't noticed before.

I closed the old book and set it on my nightstand next to my dictionary and Mr. Binkers. Then I set my alarm, turned out my light, and fell asleep.

When the alarm rang at eleven forty-five, I jumped out of bed. I was tired, but my body was up for some excitement. I changed my clothes, used the bathroom across the hall, grabbed the metal detector and a flashlight, and then made my way out of the manor. I didn't have a watch, but I made it back behind the garage before midnight.

"What are you doing?" Wyatt whispered fiercely as he sprang out from behind some trees.

Instinctively I dropped the metal detector and hit him right in the nose. He flew back howling as I tried to calm myself enough for my heart to slip back down my throat and into its proper place.

"What the heck," I breathed. "You scared me to death."

"You look plenty alive," Wyatt said holding his snout. "I think you broke my nose."

"Good. You don't spring out of the forest at someone at night."

"It was worth it," he laughed. "I bet you jumped at least six feet."

"I should have hit you harder."

I couldn't see Wyatt clearly but I could tell he was wearing a white shirt with a jacket over it. He was shorter than me with dark hair and long arms.

"So how are you?" I asked.

"I was fine up until now."

"Are you guys not getting along?" Kate asked, stepping out from around a corner of the garage.

"He hit me," Wyatt complained.

"You probably deserved it."

I liked Kate.

We walked over to where the track had been and I turned on the metal detector. It squealed like a hot microphone, sending feedback into the forest and probably waking all the animals. I adjusted the volume while Kate and Wyatt plugged their ears.

"Now that you've woken up the entire mountainside . . ." Kate complained.

"Sorry," I said. "Come on."

The metal detector gave off a low beep as I traced the track away from the back of the garage and into the forest. Wyatt was right behind me and Kate was on my left. I could see a couple of stars, but for the most part the sky was hidden by clouds. It was very dark so Kate held her flashlight so that the beam was shining directly in front of the metal detector.

"I thought we were going to see the secret room and the slide," Wyatt whined.

"We will later," I whispered. "We want to see where this goes first."

I heard something large running in the forest and stopped to make sure it wasn't running toward us.

"Must have been a deer," Kate said.

We moved again—the sound of the metal detector and our footsteps sounded in a weird, unsettling rhythm. I jammed my leg into a tree branch that I had not seen.

"Shine the light better," I complained to Kate.

Kate directed the flashlight into the air.

"Sorry," I apologized.

She moved the light back.

"So, where do you think the track goes anyway?" Wyatt asked.

"Straight," I answered, keeping the metal detector directly in front of me. We walked through the thin trees as the ground began to slope up just a bit.

"You think there's a tunnel going through the mountain?" Wyatt questioned. "Maybe there's some sort of secret place . . . with girls."

Kate and I both stopped and gave Wyatt annoyed looks.

"What? All right, then why would there be a train here?" Wyatt said defensively. "The track is covered with trees."

"There hasn't been a train on these tracks in probably a hundred years," Kate said. "The trees have grown, but the track has to go somewhere. Maybe that place is gone too . . ."

A huge deer ran right across our path. Wyatt swore while Kate dropped the flashlight and slapped me on the arm for no reason.

"Don't do that," she said.

"Do what? It's not like I asked that deer to jump in front of us."

Kate bent down and picked up her flashlight. Once again she pointed the beam of light in front of us.

My shoes crunched as I stepped over the forest floor. The track had not turned in the least. It was running perfectly straight. A tree branch swung back and smacked me in the face. When I realized there was nobody in front of me to make it swing back, I grew a little concerned.

"I think the trees are out to get me," I whispered.

"It might help if you thought about somebody besides yourself for a minute," Kate suggested.

We came to a part of the track that wasn't completely covered by dirt. I could see two wooden railroad ties and about three feet of rusted track.

"Cool," I said as Kate shined the flashlight on the track.

"We're getting close to the mountain," I whispered, although my comment was unnecessary, seeing how the ground was beginning to seriously tilt upward. "What kind of train could go up a track this steep?"

We hiked a couple of hundred feet more before the slope became too steep to continue. The metal detector still told us we were over the tracks. The side of the mountain was stone, and trees were growing sideways and at weird angles out of the cracks. Kate shined the light up and we could faintly see the track cutting between two large stone ridges and going straight up the mountain.

I was familiar with the mountain. It wasn't one I had hiked before, but it was the closest mountain to the manor. Despite that, however, I had never seen the railroad tracks on it.

"What now?" Wyatt asked.

"Let me see that," I said, reaching for the flashlight. I took it from Kate and swept the beam over the ground and the small part of the mountainside we could see. There was nothing but trees and stone.

"Shine it over there again," Kate whispered, pointing to the left of the tracks. "Above those bushes."

I moved the flashlight's beam. I could see a big bush growing right out of the base of the stone mountain.

"I don't see anything," Wyatt reported for both of us just as a thin rain began to fall. "We should go back."

"No," Kate insisted. "Look, that's a stair."

I tried to see what she saw, but I couldn't see any stairs. Kate pushed past me and pulled at the bush. A large, thick section parted, and I could easily see the stone stairs carved right into the mountain.

"Nice," I said happily.

Kate stepped through the bush. When I followed her, the foliage seemed to bristle and scratch at my already scraped-up body.

"Ouch."

"It's just a bush," Wyatt said as he stepped through scratch-free.

We started hiking up the stone stairway. After five stairs

they turned and switched up the other direction—five more stairs and it switched back again, climbing higher. The switchbacks were right next to the train track and hidden behind trees and stone ridges. At certain points you could see back down into the forest, but it was so dark I could hardly distinguish anything below.

The light rain blew into our faces.

All three of us shuffled carefully up the stairs. I was the first one to complain about how tired I was—I was also the second and third.

"You're the one who wanted to do this," Wyatt reminded me, breathing hard as we stopped for a short rest.

"Let's go just a few more steps," Kate suggested.

"Right," I agreed, and I began to slowly trudge up the next ten steps. My legs were burning, and my lungs felt like they were going to pop.

The stairs switched back a final time and then ended at the edge of a huge wall. The wall was covered in a thick layer of wet moss. I looked around. We were about halfway up the side of the mountain now. It was sort of disappointing to find nothing but moss, but it was also kind of exhilarating to reach the end of the stairs.

Kate and Wyatt began to feel around the moss for some sort of opening or door.

"It's mushy," Kate reported. "It kinda feels like wet Styrofoam."

I shined the light down at the bottom of the moss wall. I could see rusty train tracks going right under the moss.

"This has to be some sort of huge cave opening if it could fit a train," I said. "Can you push through it?"

Wyatt stepped back. He spit into both of his palms and then stamped at the ground like a charging bull. He leapt forward and jammed his right shoulder into the wall of moss. His body seemed to sink in ten inches.

"I'm stuck," he growled.

I yanked on his left arm and pulled his shoulder out. There was a wet sucking sound as he slipped free. Once he stepped back, we could see that his impact had created a large depression in the wet growth.

"Do it again," I said.

"You do it," Wyatt complained, rubbing his right arm. "This is my throwing arm."

Kate pushed at the dent mark in the moss and her fingers slipped in a few inches. She wiggled them around. It sounded like someone was playing with a chunky wad of Jell-O.

"Disgusting," she groused as she pulled her fingers back out.

"All right, move," I said with authority. I handed Kate the

flashlight and stepped back. I then rammed the moss wall with my left shoulder as hard as I could. My shoulder and upper body pushed all the way through the thick, slimy growth. The top half of me was now inside while my legs were still outside by Kate and Wyatt. I could feel one of them pulling on my legs. The moss around my torso broke away and I fell to the ground next to the train tracks. My kicking and falling made the moss opening big enough to walk through. Kate and Wyatt stepped over me as they came through the opening.

As I got back onto my feet I could hear Kate oohing and aahing at something. I stood up straight and copied her. We were standing in a huge cave. The ceiling was at least thirty feet high, and when Kate shined the light ahead we couldn't see an end to it. I saw a big metal switch on the wall and without thinking it through I pushed it up. It sparked a little and then instantly there was a humming noise followed by dim lights along the wall popping on.

"That's better," I said, trying to sound like I knew that would happen. "There must be some sort of wire leading all the way to the manor."

Wyatt was staring at me. "Are all those scratches from that bush down there?" he asked in confusion. He hadn't seen me in the light since my plant accident.

"Yeah," I lied.

We began to look around. There were some weird drawings on one side of the cave's walls, and the other side was lined with old furniture and what looked like rolled-up maps and scrolls.

The whole scene was pretty cool, but the most spectacular part was the huge metal train engine sitting on the end of the tracks. It was only one section of train, but it was tall and long. We walked all the way around it in silent awe. The front of it was sloped with a lantern hanging from it and a large cowcatcher at the bottom. It had what looked to be a thick metal roof and a long rectangle body that was divided into four sections. All four sections had windows, and there was a door with steps leading up into the front end. The whole thing looked like a combination train engine and streetcar. Behind it was a giant metal reel that was three times my height and ten feet wide with steel cable coiled on it. One end of the cable was attached to the rear of the train cart. Next to the reel was a bulky looking generator.

Above the train was a steel platform that was attached to the ground with six metal beams. One of the beams had metal rungs that someone could climb to get on top of the platform and look down at the train.

We stepped into the train. There were twelve rows of dusty seats in the back and fancy lights hanging from the ceiling. Frilly mauve curtains adorned the windows and plush, dusty rose-colored carpets were on the floor. Up front was a huge steam engine and two seats. I opened the cast-iron door where the coal was supposed to go. There were small pieces of wood stacked up and a bin full of coal next to the engine. I picked up a box of matches sitting on a short metal shelf.

"We should see if it works," I said excitedly.

"That's a really bad idea," Kate replied.

"How did this make it up that slanted track anyway?" Wyatt asked.

"It has segments," Kate said. "So it can bend like an accordion and be pulled up and lowered carefully by that cable and generator. Look at the windows. They're like six inches thick. Probably so they don't break when the cart shifts."

"I bet my dad doesn't even know this is here," I said. "And The *Grim Knot* doesn't say a thing about it. Think we can get it started?"

Kate stared at me. "That's still a bad idea."

At the back of the cave there was a giant steel door with a thick latch. I pulled the pin from the latch and lifted it. We then rolled the large door to the side. Once it was open, I could instantly see why Whitey had helped me find this place. Of course it kind of bothered me that he hadn't just said to look for a train track and hike up to a cave.

Behind the door was a massive cavern lit by a couple dozen

bare lightbulbs hanging by the walls. This cavern was twice the size of the front one and as large as two indoor football fields put side to side. The ceiling was at least fifty feet high. All around the room there were wooden crates and hundreds of barrels. On one of the edges was a small, round spring filled with crystal clear water. And in the middle of the room, I saw four wooden posts that looked just like the ones that had once been in the conservatory. Next to each post was a short, leafy plant with thick, black leaves.

"This whole mountain's hollow," Wyatt said, impressed.

On the far end was a small, wooden door as well as a huge iron cage that fit into a carved-out side of the cave. We walked over to the wooden door and pulled it open. There was nothing but a long, dark tunnel behind it.

We ignored the tunnel for the moment and checked out the humongous cage. The bars were so tall and wide that we could easily slip between them. There was a giant-sized door with a pin in the lock.

We opened a couple of the wooden barrels and found they were filled with some sort of dry, cereal-looking stuff. Wyatt tried one and said they tasted like bark. We also looked into some of the crates. There was rope in one and old clothes in another. One was filled with ornate table lamps and fancy china.

Kate walked over to the four posts sticking out of the center of the massive cavern. Wyatt and I followed her. She touched one of the posts and then knelt down by the plant.

"These plants look different from the last ones," she said, brushing the leaves.

"How do they even grow in this dark place?" I asked.

"You tell me," she said. "You're the one with the freaky plant connection."

"They're kinda cool-looking," Wyatt spoke up. "I've never seen a plant with black leaves and white edges."

Kate stood up and faced me. "So you're supposed to find the stone and raise the dragon in here?"

"What?" Wyatt asked in surprise. "You still have one of those stones?"

I looked at Wyatt. His wet, dark hair was plastered to his head. The raindrops on his face made it look as though he had been crying.

Nobody besides my father and Kate knew about the single stone that had been produced when Pip had died. Well, that really white guy suspected, but he didn't know for sure. I had kept the secret from Wyatt because I knew that if it ever got out we'd have people combing the mountains looking for it.

"Do you have another stone?" Wyatt persisted.

"Maybe."

"That'll grow a dragon?"

I nodded.

"And you didn't tell me?" he yelled.

"He told me," Kate said, making things worse.

"I couldn't," I insisted. "It's too dangerous. You know what those last stones did."

Wyatt had been the one to help me fight off some of the dragons. I had found him in Kingsplot where the dragons were pillaging. He had been hiding under a bench. Together we had destroyed most of the beasts.

"I know what they did," Wyatt said, sounding hurt.

"My father made me promise not to tell."

"You told Kate," he reminded me.

"He did," Kate said proudly.

"Would you stop exacerbating the situation?" I asked her, unconsciously using one of my new dictionary words as my voice echoed off the cavern walls. "Who cares when I told you, Wyatt? What matters is that now we have to find that stone and hatch the dragon so I can finish it."

"What matters is that I get back home," Kate said. "My parents will be waking up in a couple of hours, and I can't . . . wait . . . do you hear that?"

"Hear what?" I asked quietly.

"It's like a whistling, breathing sort of noise," she said. "Do you hear it?"

"That's just Wyatt," I told her. "His nose hums when he breathes."

"It's true," Wyatt admitted. "I'm going to get my adenoids . . ."

"Shhhhhhh," Kate demanded. "Listen."

I could hear something now. It sounded a bit like wind being sucked through a straw while the straw was being flapped around wildly.

"It's coming from that door we opened," I said nervously while pointing across the massive cavern to the far end.

"We should go," Wyatt said, definitely scared now.

"We've gotta close the door," I replied.

It was too late, the noise grew louder. Suddenly, huge bursts of what looked like thick, gray dust exploded from the openings. The gray cloud raced across the room, blocking lights and rolling toward us. Wyatt was already running for the front of the cave.

"Go!" I hollered.

"What is it?" Kate screamed back.

"I think they're . . ." I was going to say bats, I mean, we were in a cave after all, but just then millions of thick, dusty moths swarmed around me, and I changed my guess. I started to yell something else, but some flew into my mouth, flapping their feathery, duster-like wings. There were so many they pushed me to the ground. It was a struggle to get back up.

"It must . . . the lights." I barely heard Kate screech.

Her words were buried by the vibrating hum of millions of moth wings flapping. It was hard to see anything besides dark dots, but I stumbled in what I believed was the direction of the large metal door. I felt Kate bump up against the side of me, and I grabbed her arm. The moths were clinging to my face in thick patches. I could feel them working down into my shirt and moving up my pant legs. A hot and painful panic filled my body—I honestly never thought I'd die by moth.

I reached the wall and felt around with my free hand as I tried to see through all the moths. I found the door opening. I could feel, and faintly see, the horde of moths swarming through the huge opening like a dirty river, into the large front cavern where the train was.

Kate fell to the ground, and I jerked her up as we pushed through the thick moths toward the moss wall. I didn't know where Wyatt was or if he had already made it out. We reached the train and pulled ourselves forward as the moths swirled in great bulky patterns that batted us back and forth. My arms were covered and it felt like I was wearing a bug turban on top of my head. The noise was deafening, and it caused my brain to rattle around in my head.

The opening in the moss wall was much larger now that all the moths were moving out of it. Holding Kate's hand, I got out of the cave and over to the stairs on the left side of the opening. Instantly the bugs thinned and I could see my arms and the stairs clearly. I looked back and viewed the stream of moths pouring out of the opening and moving into the dark night.

Kate was spitting and frantically whacking at her hair. I pulled my shirt off and started slapping my legs and back with it. I was tempted to take off my pants because there were hundreds of squirming bugs in them, but I was coherent enough to realize that if we survived this, Kate would tease me endlessly for wearing boxers that had dogs on them.

"Where's Wyatt?" I yelled while digging moths out of my ears.

"He's still in there," Kate said, worried. "We have to get him."

"Did you see all those things?" I wailed.

Kate was already moving back toward the moss opening. The insects were still swarming out of the cave. Thousands of them were as big as mice and millions were as small as Tic-Tacs with wings. Random beams of light shot out like lasers through the moths.

"You've got to go in and turn the lights off," Kate said.

I looked around. "Me?"

"Yeah," Kate replied. "Then maybe they'll settle down."

"But . . ."

"They won't kill you," Kate argued.

"Then Wyatt should be fine," I argued back.

It was rainy and dark, and I couldn't really see Kate all that clearly, but I knew exactly the kind of look she was giving me.

"All right," I gave in. I figured since I still had them down my pants and in my hair I might as well do it. I waved my shirt like a helicopter and charged back into the opening. Moths splattered up against me like fat drops of water. One shot right into my mouth. I gagged and spit it out.

I got to the wall and groped around for the switch. The second I found it I threw it down, and the lights went off. The only light now came from the opening in the moss that showed a tiny sliver of the slightly less-dark outside world. The bugs began to head to the dim light and out of the cave.

I knelt down and covered my head. It seemed like forever before most of them were gone. I lifted my hands off of my head and looked around in the dark. I could see dots of them going out, but it seemed there were fewer in the cave.

I stood up. "Wyatt!"

I heard something call from the direction of the train. I held my arms in front of me and felt my way to the train.

"Wyatt!"

"Here!" he yelled back.

I felt for the door and then climbed up the few steps into

the train. Moths kept hitting me on the face and arms, but the amount was bearable now.

"Wyatt!"

He shouted back, and I found him down on the floor hiding between two rows of train seats. He was shaking as I helped him up.

"You won't tell any girls that I hid?" he asked worriedly as I helped him up.

"Probably not," I answered, as if I actually spoke to any girls ever about anything.

"I just wanted to see the secret room," he moaned.

"Sorry," I apologized. "I thought you loved trains."

"Not anymore."

I helped Wyatt out of the train, and we left the cave as fast as we could. Kate was almost completely moth free and she helped swat bugs off Wyatt and me.

By the time I got home it was four-thirty in the morning. There was no way I could go straight to bed, so I took a shower and discovered smashed moths in places on my body that no moth should ever go.

After my shower I laid down in bed. My mind was racing a thousand miles an hour as I thought about what we had found and what it all meant. A hidden cave, a rusty old train with tracks that lead right up to the garage—it was all pretty confusing. I wanted my dad to be here so I could find out what he knew. I thought my mind was really buzzing, but I realized it was just a tiny moth in my ear.

"You've got to be kidding." I quickly flicked it out.

I fell asleep to the sound of roosters crowing.

Illustration from page 19 of The Grim Knot

CHAPTER 10

Rock It

B Y THE TIME I WOKE UP, it technically was no longer Sunday morning. It was just after noon, and sunshine was streaming through my window. When I looked out, I couldn't see a single cloud. Because the weather around the manor was usually overcast and wet, a truly clear day made everything amazing.

Millie chastised me for sleeping in and called me overindulgent. She then fed me the biggest lunch I had ever eaten. My father still hadn't come back, and Millie was extremely concerned about it.

"He never leaves the manor," she worried.

"He left a note," I reminded her. "If he was in trouble, he would have just disappeared."

Millie put a large slice of coconut cream pie on my plate

and then sprinkled it with roasted coconut flakes. When she failed to offer me ice cream with it, I could tell that she was really upset.

"Maybe you should take a vacation," I said kindly.

Millie stared at me. "Now what would I do with time off? I'd just sit around and worry even more about you and your father."

"But wouldn't it be more fun to worry about us if you were on a beach vacationing?"

"I burn easily," Millie said as if that settled it.

I had wisely made plans to meet Kate and Wyatt near the field filled with boulders at two o'clock. So I still had a little time to myself. I ran back up to my floor and over to the south wing. I went through the small green door and slid open the mirror. The thin stairway was dark, but not as dark as before. I could see little cracks of light at the top of the walls and some slipping in under the bottom of them. I closed the mirror behind me and climbed the stairs.

I made it to the top of the slide and looked down. I could see the actual slide better. It was a highly polished wood, and the ceiling was so low I couldn't believe I had made it down without severely hurting myself. There were torn cobwebs everywhere.

"I survived last time," I told myself as I sat down and pushed off.

The ride was much more enjoyable when I could sort of see. I flew around one of the corners and my right leg twisted throwing me down a different track. I hadn't seen the fork in the slide the other night, but I could tell from all the intact cobwebs that nobody had been on the stretch I was now zipping down for quite some time. I whizzed around a sharp corner and then down a long dip. My shoulders bashed against the walls and my hands kept hitting the ceiling.

The slide came to an abrupt end in a long, skinny room with high walls. As I slowly stood up, I saw a small piece of wood about eye level hanging on one of the walls. I slid the wood to the side and there were two small peepholes. I looked through them, and I could see into one of the lavish rooms on the bottom floor in the main wing. It was a closed-off room and most of the furniture was covered with white sheets. It was actually one of the more furnished rooms. So many pieces of furniture from the manor had been sold by Millie and Thomas to pay for taxes when they thought they were in charge of the bills. Once my father explained to them that there was money in places they didn't know about, the selling of furniture had ceased.

I slid the tiny board that covered the eyeholes back into

place and began searching the small, narrow room for some way out. I was just about to try climbing back up the slide when I noticed that one of the boards on the wall had an indentation in it about waist high. I stuck one of my thumbs into the indentation and a lower section of the wall slid to the side. I crawled through the opening and out into the large room. The door was actually part of the room's dark wood wainscoting and once it was moved back into place I could hardly tell where it was. I found a small thumbhole on the baseboard that let me open it back up, and I studied the location for a few minutes.

I stood up and looked at the portrait above me on the wall. It was a painting of a lady with a high feathery hat and wrinkly eyes. As I looked at her closely, I saw that the peepholes I had found in the adjoining room were right where her eyes were. I hadn't slid the board all the way back into place so she sort of looked like a loon. A small, gold plaque on the bottom of the frame said, "Lady Harrington."

I left the room and went down a long hall and out one of the rear doors. The back gardens had once been completely overgrown but now Scott kept up a large section directly behind the manor. Sunshine spread across the trees and the mountains like butter. The simile probably would have made me hungry, but I was stuffed from lunch.

By the time I got to the boulder fields Kate was there

waiting. I thought she would have a hard time getting away from her house, but she said her parents were in town. As usual she looked bored and considerably older than sixteen.

"Think Wyatt will come?" I asked.

"I don't know," she answered. "He was pretty shaken up last night."

I gazed out over the rockslide. It was an amazing sight. It looked like a massive stone river flowing from the middle of the mountains all the way down into the valley—with the sun out, all the rocks sparkled brilliantly. There were rocks of all sizes, but the majority of the stones were about the size of the one I had thrown into them so many months ago.

"Maybe we should start without Wyatt," I suggested. "This might take a while."

"You think?" Kate asked. "What area did you throw it in?"

I re-created my steps on that fateful day. "The last dragon had just been killed and the stone dropped," I narrated. "I picked up the stone and ran through those trees. I got to the edge of the stone field and was about to throw it when my father stopped me. We talked and then I threw it right over there."

"Did you see where it landed?"

"I turned around so I wouldn't see," I told her.

"How noble," Kate said. "How far do you think it went?"

I shrugged. Kate picked up a rock from the ground and handed it to me.

"Thanks," I said politely, wishing somebody would actually give me a good gift.

Kate shook her head. "No, if you throw that as hard as you threw the stone, it will help us figure out where it might have fallen."

I moved to where I thought I had been standing all those months ago. "I'm not sure this is a good idea," I said. "It won't be completely accurate because I'm probably stronger than I was then."

"Give me a break," Kate said. "Throw it."

The stone I was holding was actually pretty heavy. I swung my arms and then threw it. I turned around so I wouldn't see it fall.

"Why are you turned around?" Kate laughed.

"Oh yeah," I said, embarrassed. "Did you see where it went?"

Kate nodded her head and pointed. It looked like she was pointing only a few feet away.

"It had to go further than that," I asserted.

"Maybe you're weaker now," she suggested.

"Funny, get me another rock."

Kate handed me a second rock and I threw it as hard as I

could. This time I didn't look away. It wasn't a very impressive throw either.

"Let's just start looking," I suggested.

We slowly began to walk through the rocks searching for the one I had thrown originally. The rocks all looked so similar. I tried to feel as many as I could, hoping the real rock would glow under my touch.

"Is this it?" Kate asked, holding up a stone.

"No," I said. "The end's too square."

"Maybe it got chipped off when you dropped it," Kate said.

"I didn't drop it, I threw it."

"Right," Kate smiled.

I walked over and touched the rock she was holding. It didn't glow. After about half an hour I started to get depressed. I thought it would be a little easier to find, but I was starting to see stones that weren't even there. The sunshine didn't help either, it just made the rocks look like billions of bleached bumps.

I was about to complain some more when I felt someone tap my shoulder. I turned around expecting to see Wyatt, but instead I saw nothing but a tree.

"Um, Kate," I said as she continued looking down at the stones. "Kate!"

Kate looked over toward me and gasped.

One of the tallest trees on the edge of the stone field was bending over. A long branch near the bottom of it was poking me. I stepped back and my left foot got wedged in between two stones. As I pulled it out, I lost my balance and fell hard on my rear. My teeth bit down on my tongue.

"Aawuch."

Kate was now standing behind me, and we both were staring up at the bending tree. It was tall and curved like a rainbow. Kate and I scooted back. It creaked and chirped as it further contorted itself. Squirrels and birds were leaping out of the branches and scrambling down the arched trunk.

"Unbelievable," Kate whispered.

I was pretty impressed, but after all the things I had seen since I had moved to Kingsplot, it wasn't actually *unbelievable* to me.

The top of the tree bent further and further until it was two feet from the ground. It thrust its crown forward, reaching for something.

"What the heck is it doing?" I whispered.

Kate was too in awe to answer. So we both watched in silence as the tree extended some of its upper branches to stretch even farther.

"It's trying to get something," I said.

The tree was bent over as far as it could, reaching over the river of rock. The longest top branch extended from the top of the tree by a good three feet. The thin branch shook and wiggled trying to reach farther. The tree's roots began to slowly pull up from the dirt as it stretched and lengthened.

"It's looking for the stone," I said in amazement. "It wants us to find it."

I stood up, and both of us stepped carefully toward where the top of the tree was. It yanked its roots out a couple of more inches. The long top branch lowered just a bit more and gently touched the back of a single stone that was half buried by other small boulders.

Kate pushed me forward and I bent down to get the rock. The tree kept its branch on it until I had picked it up.

Instantly the stone glowed in my hands. I felt chills running from the bottom of my feet up into my forehead. I held the stone in one hand and reached out to pet the top of the tree with my other.

"Thanks," I whispered.

"It's not a dog," Kate pointed out.

The tree creaked and wriggled and then with one loud slap, it sprang back up. A squirrel that had not been wise enough to get off went flying through the air as the tree wobbled to a stiff stop.

"That was helpful," Kate said, staring at the once again tall tree.

"They've been so mean to me lately."

"I think they just wanted you to do what you're supposed to."

Wyatt came running out of the forest and stopped at the edge of the rocks. He was breathing hard and his hair was sweaty.

"Sorry I'm late," he heaved. "You already found it?"

Kate and I both nodded.

"Was it hard to find?" he asked.

"Not really," I answered.

We made our way back to the manor watching out for signs of anyone else. Just to be nice, I let Wyatt carry the heavy stone so he could feel needed.

I'm not sure he appreciated it as much as I thought he should.

Illustration from page 20 of The Grim Knot

CHAPTER 11

Don't Stop Me

W E PLACED THE STONE IN THE water beneath the twisted snake statue. Then I took Kate and Wyatt inside. I showed them the cool little green door and we went through the mirror and hiked up the slender, winding staircase. When we got to the top of the slide I warned them about staying to the right if they saw a fork. I also told them that if they ended up in the other room they should just look through the painting until I got there.

Kate practically jumped down the slide, and, after waiting a few moments, Wyatt followed. I took my turn, and when I reached the end, they were both standing there begging to go again.

"You could travel anywhere in this house without anybody knowing," Kate said excitedly. "Let's go again."

It was tempting, but I knew we had to get back to the cave while it was still daylight. Wyatt wanted to opt out, but after I promised him he could just wait outside of the cave, he agreed to go.

We retrieved the stone from the fountain and I put it inside a backpack. It was heavy, but not half as bad as actually carrying it with my hands. I definitely preferred hiking through the woods during the day versus trudging through them at night. We made much better time and the trees didn't attack me like they had before.

When we reached the side of the mountain where the stairs began, we all grumbled, but we knew there was no easier way.

"Actually," Wyatt said. "If I'm just going to wait at the top of the stairs, I might as well just wait at the bottom."

We made fun of him until he agreed to at least climb up with us. The stone stairs were very cool. I hadn't been able to see too much of them last night so it was amazing to take them all in. They were carved right into the side of the mountain and covered by trees that grew sideways out of the stone wall. The trees did a fantastic job of hiding the stairs and the train tracks that ran up the slope of the mountain. On the side of the stairs were tiny carvings of small gargoyle-like beings that were pointing in different directions.

Halfway up the stairs I gave Wyatt the backpack to carry.

I offered it to Kate first but she declined. When we reached the moss wall we were all breathing hard. The section of moss growing on the stone was at least twenty feet high and fifteen feet wide. And the hole we had made last night was about the size of a car standing up on its back end. I looked through the opening carefully.

"Any moths?" Wyatt asked.

"Only dead ones," I said, pointing to the ground.

"Good," Wyatt cheered. "After what they did to me on the train, they don't deserve to live."

The light from outdoors pushed in through the opening and lit the front cavern up pretty well. I could see the train and it looked like a giant metal monster that was sound asleep.

"Come on, Kate," I waved.

Kate and I walked over to the train. We were kicking up dead moths and the sound of our shuffling bounced off the high stone walls. We walked back to the large steel door. Kate was holding onto my right arm, and I could see Wyatt right beside me. I stopped, and we all slammed into each other.

"What are you doing?" Wyatt asked.

"I thought you were going to wait outside," I said.

"It's the kid that waits outside who always gets eaten," Wyatt explained.

"Yeah, that was our plan," I said, walking again. I stopped after three steps.

"What now?" Kate asked.

"Well, since the lights aren't on, the back cavern is going to be pretty dark," I informed her.

"Just go," Kate said. "We'll close the door to the tunnel and then we can come back and turn the lights on."

I knew the plan, I just wasn't totally happy about having to walk through the huge, dark cavern. Luckily it wasn't as black as I thought it would be. The large open door gave all the boxes and obstacles some definition. We made it to the back, closed the tunnel door, and slid the bolt into place. Kate noticed a switch near the back tunnels and, when she threw it on, the place lit up.

"Wow, this room is huge," I said in wonder.

I unzipped the backpack and took the stone out. It glowed in my hand like one of the dim lights on the walls.

"Are you sure about this?" Wyatt asked, actually being the voice of reason for the first time in his life.

"I don't think I have a choice," I replied. "The trees will beat me up if I don't."

"It'll just grow one dragon, right?" Kate asked. "That's it?"

I nodded, pretending I was an expert on the subject. "That old guy said it'll be the queen."

"Will she have a crown?" Wyatt asked seriously.

Kate and I both stared at him.

"What?" he said defensively. "I don't know anything about queen dragons."

"Obviously," Kate smiled.

"All right," I said with just a touch of nervousness. "I'll plant it now."

All three of us just stood there.

"Go on," Kate finally said as she nudged me forward.

I didn't move.

"Don't even try to stop me," I insisted.

Wyatt took a turn nudging me. I'm not completely sure why I was so hesitant. Ever since I had killed the last dragon I had wanted to see another one. They were amazing, and the time Kate and I had spent with them provided some of the most incredible moments of my life. But I also knew what they could do. Not only could they tear apart houses and light buildings on fire, they also had the ability to make my family even crazier. My family's history was filled with the ill effects that dragons and their power had on us. The women had gone mad. My own father had exiled himself to the top of the manor just so he wouldn't be tempted to abuse the power. I knew it was in my blood to use them for the wrong reasons, and I was more than just a little concerned about that. I wanted to be a better person, and I wasn't sure this was a step in the right direction.

"Are you going to do it?" Kate asked.

I kept hearing Whitey's voice in my head.

"Seven days."

I figured at least two of those seven days had already passed so I changed the voice in my head to say, *"Five days."*

I had no time to waste. I walked to the center of the massive room and up to one of the wicked-looking plants growing out of the ground. I looked at the stone in my hand and made a wish. I knew it wasn't a wishing stone, but I figured it couldn't hurt. I bent over and placed the rock on the soil.

I stood up and turned to look at Kate.

"Are you sure this is a good idea?" I asked.

She shrugged her shoulders, more, I think, out of complete uncertainty than boredom.

I looked back at the stone. It sank slowly into the soil a couple of inches, and the plant beside it was still. I gazed directly at the small plant and did what I knew I had to do.

"Grow," I commanded it.

Almost instantly the plant began to shiver. Its leaves shook, and a small black shoot shot out of the middle like a serpent's tongue. It twisted up then arched itself down into the dirt. Two seconds later it popped up next to the stone and quickly wrapped itself around it. The stone glowed for a moment as the shoot thickened and covered the entire rock. The plant settled and seemed to exhale.

"Creepy," Wyatt whispered. "What now?"

"We wait."

We walked away from the plant, and all three of us took some time looking through crates and then checking out the cave. Eventually we all ended up in the train.

"This train could work again," I said excitedly.

"There are trees growing in the track," Kate reminded us.

"Still, we could at least start it up."

Wyatt agreed with me, but Kate never saw the logic. By the time we left the cave, the sun was just beginning to slide down. The sunset was as spectacular as any I had ever seen above Kingsplot, and it almost seemed that for that moment nothing could go wrong.

It's funny how moments like that don't last very long.

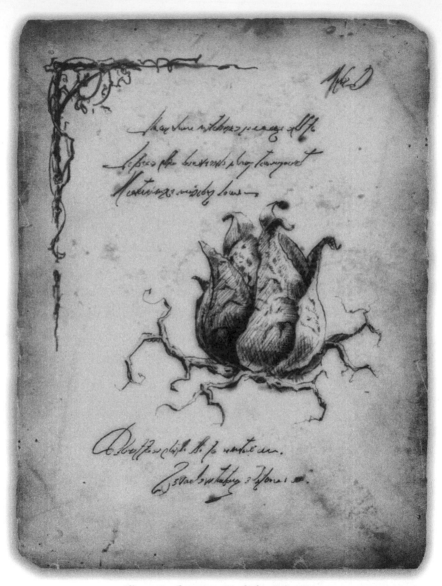

Illustration from page 22 of The Grim Knot

CHAPTER 12

Life Is Pretty Real

I'M NOT A COMPLETE FOOL. I mean I know I was wrong for blowing up that weather balloon and destroying the shop shed. Yet for some reason, I expected more of a welcome return when I stepped off of the school bus and onto the Callowbrow campus for the first time since the incident. After I had killed the dragons, everyone had treated me like a hero. Now, they all just ignored me, except for one of the older boys who nailed me on the side of my head with a donut.

"Just ignore him," Kate said as we both walked to the front doors. "He's just mad that he has to take ballroom dance now instead of shop."

"I don't blame him," I said while wiping frosting off of my face. "I'd wanna beat myself up too."

We walked through the front doors and split up. A short

girl who was a couple of years younger than me stuck her tongue out and stared at me as I put things into my locker.

I finally said. "Your tongue's going to dry out."

"You broke my finger," she replied angrily.

"Sorry."

"A part of the shed you blew up hit my finger and broke it."

"Still sorry," I added.

"I can't make it go straight," she complained, holding up her right hand to show me that her middle finger was in a splint. "I have to write with my left hand."

"I'm no longer sorry," I told her, closing my locker and walking away.

First period was Professor Squall's class. He was an older guy with thick hair and bushy eyebrows, one of which was higher than the other and gave him a look of constant suspicion. He had a tiny button nose and was wearing a tweed jacket. He and I were a lot friendlier ever since I had found out that he was once engaged to Francine, the woman who had raised me.

"Beck," he said coldly as he came into class. "Glad to see you're feeling well. There's a lot of work you'll need to catch up on. What say we meet after class?"

I tried to look excited.

Wyatt came in and took a seat next to me. "Finally," he said. "This looks right. It's been pretty boring here without you."

"Thanks," I said sincerely, happy that someone was being nice to me. "Everyone's pretty upset with me."

Wyatt shrugged. "Whatever, wait 'til that new dragon you planted grows," he whispered. "Then they'll really hate you."

Professor Squall taught us about simple machinery. He went on and on about ropes and mechanisms and how pulling something one way can lift and pull things another way. He then assigned us a bunch of homework and challenged us to make our own pulley or simple machine. He excused everybody except me.

"Beck," he said loudly. "Remember, I need to see you."

"Good luck," Wyatt laughed, grabbing his books and slipping out.

As soon as everyone was gone, Professor Squall walked up the stairs and told me to follow. I did so, and soon we were in his office with the door closed.

"Have a seat, Beck."

I sat down in a wooden chair in front of his messy desk. He sat down in a padded leather one behind it.

"Simple machinery is fascinating, isn't it?" he asked.

"Can't wait to make my own pulley," I replied.

"Excellent. You know I was tempted to come and visit you in the hospital," he smiled.

"Tempted?" I asked, thinking it was a weird word to use.

"Let's just say I didn't want to bump into your father."

I laughed. "There was no chance of that happening."

"Are you all right?" he asked.

"Fine," I answered.

"Still a little scraped up, I see."

The wounds from the plant attack were almost gone, but there were still some traces of them on my arms and forehead. "Just a little."

"The school's asked me to talk with you," he said uncomfortably. "There are more than a few people concerned about things."

"I forget, how many is a few?"

Professor Squall didn't laugh.

"You know tearing apart the shed was not a good idea," he said sternly.

"For the record, I didn't mean to tear it apart," I argued. "I thought it was just a big ball. I'm really sorry."

"That almost sounds sincere," he replied.

I wanted to get mad at him for not taking me seriously, but I knew that it was my own fault that I had such a rotten reputation.

"Beck, you've acted foolishly," Professor Squall said. "Your family still has a tremendous amount of pull around here. It's no secret how much wealth your father has, despite the amount of land he had to sell off and restitution he had to make to fix what happened. You can't afford to mess up any further. Do you understand?"

"Some things," I answered honestly.

Professor Squall sighed. "Please keep your nose clean."

I was suddenly self-conscious about my nostrils.

"There's a limit to what people can tolerate," he added. "One more strike and you might very well find yourself in water that's too hot to swim in."

"Like a hot tub?"

"Beck," he scolded.

"I'll be careful," I said wiping at my nose.

"Just act like a normal boy," he suggested. "I understand what it feels like to rebel, but find a better outlet—play stickball, whistle at girls . . . I don't know, chew gum in the bathroom."

He really didn't know what it was like to be a rebel.

"Is that it?" I asked as the bell rang for the next hour.

"One more thing," he said. "A man was by to see you."

"A white man?" I asked excitedly.

Professor Squall looked confused. "I suppose he was white."

"What did he want?"

"He asked a lot of questions about you. I think he wants to write an article about how you are now."

"Oh," I said disappointed. "Was he a reporter?"

Professor Squall nodded.

"That's not the white man I was talking about," I sighed. "If that reporter comes around again, don't tell him anything."

"Of course," Professor Squall said. "Besides, I already told him everything I knew."

I put my head in my hands.

"Just be careful," he continued. "Reporters have a way of taking what you say and twisting it around."

"Well, then it's a good thing you told him everything." My neck was burning. "Thanks a lot."

"You're welcome," he replied.

"I don't believe this."

"You should. This is real life, Beck," he whispered fiercely. "There's no more playing around. Do you understand?"

I shook my head. "Got it."

"Go on," Professor Squall said. "I'll write you a slip to excuse the tardy."

"Good," I smiled. "Because I think I'm going to go chew some gum in the bathroom."

"Did you not hear a word I said?" he asked.

"But, you told me to whistle at girls and stuff."

"You are hopeless," he grumbled as he scribbled out a tardy slip for my next class, "absolutely hopeless."

I stood up, walked off, and wished that I lived in a world where the things adults said made sense to me.

Illustration from page 25 of The Grim Knot

CHAPTER 13

Father to Son

K ATE AND I CHECKED ON THE stone almost every day. My legs were getting much stronger due to climbing so many stairs. We had thoroughly investigated the two big caverns, but we had not opened the tunnel door back up. Occasionally a swarm of moths would come in through the moss opening, but never enough to worry us.

I don't know what it was, but for some reason I loved cleaning the cavern. It was torture for me to have to make my bed back in the manor, but in the cavern I was constantly polishing the train, organizing boxes, and straightening things up. I loved to climb up on the platform that was over the train and look down through the steel grates. I liked looking directly into the smokestack and walking the length of the engine from above.

The stone I had planted had completely disappeared into a leafy cocoon and the cocoon was growing bigger every day.

Kate, Wyatt, and I had debated over whether Whitey had meant the stone would hatch in seven days or if he meant that it had needed to be planted in seven days. But after eight days and it still hadn't hatched we figured he meant planted. We liked to sit around the cocoon and listen to it gurgle while talking about how we had saved the world by planting it in time.

"I guess we avoided a catastrophe," I said proudly.

"Maybe," Kate said. "I'm more worried about the catastrophe that will happen when it hatches."

"So what was it like?" Wyatt asked. "I mean you guys took care of those dragons before they messed up Kingsplot."

"Those were kind of cool days," I admitted. "I never had too many friends back home so it was nice to just hang out with Kate and Milo and witness dragons growing up."

"It was pretty weird and unbelievable," Kate added. "Almost surreal."

"And you never suspected Milo wasn't Milo?"

"Nope," Kate and I said in unison.

"You had names for the dragons, didn't you?" Wyatt asked. We both nodded.

"So what about this one?" he asked. "It's a girl, right? So, we should probably think up a name."

We were all silent for a moment as we thought.

"I like the name Kara," Wyatt suggested.

We both just stared at him.

"What?" he said insecurely.

"Like the Kara at our school?" I asked.

"There's a Kara at our school?"

"Yeah, you know, the one you're always talking about," Kate reminded him. "The one you sent a present to on her birthday."

"Her name's Kara?" Wyatt questioned innocently.

"You have it written all over your folders," I reminded him.

"And you made that song up," Kate added. "What was it called, 'Kara Time'?"

Wyatt was good and red in the face now. "Oh yeah, I remember now. I think her name is Kara."

"You're so pathetic," I said.

"So, then what would you name it?" Wyatt asked.

"How about 'Kate'?" I suggested.

Kate shook her head. "I can't believe I like you."

"What? I've always thought that was a great name," I said defensively. "It means pure."

"How do you know what it means?" she asked.

"I might have accidentally looked it up."

"And you say I'm pathetic?" Wyatt argued.

I thought Kate was going to make fun of me some more

but instead she leaned over and rested her head on my shoulder. I'm pretty confident I will never understand girls.

As we exited the cave, I took a moment to stand on the top of the stone stairway and look out from between the trees. Clouds were spreading over the blue sky making it look like Mother Nature was pulling up a big white comforter. I could see way down into the valley where Kingsplot sat surrounded by blue lakes and deep green trees. I gazed at the manor. The copper dome on top looked gold under the new clouds. I couldn't see too clearly because of the distance, but I thought I saw a shadow moving around in the dome.

"I think my dad's back," I said excitedly. "Look."

Wyatt looked around confused.

"No, down on top of the manor."

I didn't wait around to see if they understood me. Instead I started down the stairs as fast as I could. I needed to talk to my dad.

"What're you doing?" Kate asked as she jogged down the stairs behind me.

"I gotta talk to my dad," I huffed. "Have Wyatt take you home."

"I don't need anyone to take me home," she said bothered and considerably less out of breath than me.

Kate passed me on the stairs and took off. I tried to keep

up, but I wanted her to feel good about herself so I let her get way out in front of me. When I reached the bottom of the stone stairs she was so far ahead of me that I could no longer see her. I felt bad, but at least Wyatt was still behind me.

I took a few moments to rest near the scratchy bush, allowing Wyatt to catch up to me. His breathing was way more labored than mine.

"What the heck," he gasped. "Why couldn't you have found a secret cave with an escalator?"

The two of us half-jogged and half-walked as fast as we could to the back of the garage house. From there Wyatt took off, and I ran to the manor. Millie was in the kitchen humming and making some sort of pastry.

"Is that strudel?" I asked happily.

Millie nodded—strudel was my father's favorite dessert.

"So he's home?"

"Up where he should be," Millie smiled. "He rang me earlier."

I took the seven flights of stairs as quickly as I could. By the time I got to the door leading into the dome I was exhausted. I knocked, pushed open the door, and climbed in. My father was looking through his telescope toward the valley.

"Dad!"

"Beck," he said, without looking away from the telescope.

"It was such a clear day. I could see the large cathedral down in Kingsplot, but the clouds are back now."

"That's lovely," I said, annoyed. "Where were you?"

"Not important," he replied, finally turning from the telescope.

"I've needed to talk to you," I informed him. "I don't know if you remember this, but you have a son."

Aeron shifted and looked me directly in the eyes. His face looked tired and drawn. He tried to smile and then waved as if that would have to do for now.

"Sorry," he said exhaling. "I still have no idea how to act like a father."

"Or a normal person," I helped him. "Normal people don't hide themselves away and then leave a note when they take off for days without giving more information."

"Which one of us is the dad?" my father asked. "You might be a loose bolt, but sometimes you amaze me."

There was a compliment in there somewhere, and I liked it.

"That man came back," I told him.

"Who came back?" my dad asked anxiously.

"Whitey," I clarified. "Did you know there are secret passages in the manor?"

"What are you talking about?"

I told my father everything I could possibly remember

about Mr. Ashen. I told him about the secret passageway and the slide and the painting that looked out.

"Just like in the movies," I said excitedly.

I told him about how I only had seven days and how the trees had been picking on me. I went into depth about finding the railroad tracks that led right into the garage house, and I gave him the lowdown on the cave.

"So that's why I hate moths now," I said.

"I suppose I don't blame you," my father replied. I could see from the storm in his eyes that he was trying to digest all the things I had just told him.

"I didn't know what to do," I admitted. "You were gone and Whitey was so insistent that I acted quickly."

My father just stood there.

"Do you know him?" I asked. "Should we trust him?"

My father looked up. "Yes, I know him."

"And?"

"Our family is mad," my father said needlessly.

"That's not comforting," I complained.

"I shouldn't have come back," he said in a panic.

"What?"

"I was wrong to return," he insisted. "I was wrong to come back. This is a mistake, Beck. I have to go."

I was so flabbergasted I could barely be sarcastic. Somehow I managed. "You want me to help you pack?"

"Yes, grab that book," he said, pointing at a large weathered atlas.

"No way," I shouted. "I was joking. You can't just go."

"I must."

"Why?"

"You don't understand, Beck," he said, flustered.

"I really don't," I replied. "Tell me what's going on. What do I do?"

"I can't help you here," he told me. "There's too much at stake."

"So what do I do?"

He shrugged.

"I can't believe it," I moaned.

He didn't seem to even hear me.

"I must go." He grabbed his leather satchel and shoved the atlas into it. He then threw open the door to the stairs.

"You can't run away," I argued. "I need you."

My father looked torn between the thoughts in his head and the instructions of his heart.

"It's all I know," he said with shame.

"What about the strudel?" I asked disgustedly.

My father turned to look at me. "Tell Millie I'm sorry."

"Well, what about me?"

He looked me in the eyes again, and I could see that the storm was building. "I love you, Beck," he said kindly, and with that he was gone.

I just stood there. I tried to recall every word my father had ever said to me in the past. I think one time he admitted that he liked me, and he may have said he wasn't bothered that I was around, but, "I love you?" If he wasn't so complexly flighty and confusing, I would have almost been touched.

I looked out the dome windows and watched the wind pick up. It had been quite some time since I had felt so alone. It started to rain and the fat drops beat down upon the copper dome like small, flat rocks.

I couldn't believe it.

I climbed down the stairs and made my way to the kitchen. Millie was still there, but instead of humming she was grumbling.

"What happened?" she asked, her one crooked eye looking over my left shoulder. "He ran out of the manor."

"I have no idea," I replied. "We were talking and he freaked out."

"Something's not right," she said sadly.

I couldn't have agreed more—my stomach felt like it was

going to implode. In fact I was so uncomfortable that it took everything I had to finish off three full helpings of strudel.

Lightning and thunder struck, and the new rain turned into a torrential downpour.

Illustration from page 27 of The Grim Knot

CHAPTER 14

Rain Must Fall

I WAS PRETTY USED TO IT RAINING in the Hagen Valley. It didn't rain that terribly often where I had come from, but here it was a rare day that didn't include some sort of drizzle. We were currently, however, experiencing so much rain I was beginning to think that I should start building an ark.

The rain just wouldn't let up.

Kingsplot was becoming a lake, and the mountains that surrounded us were experiencing incredible mudslides and flooding. Huge waterfalls were running off the sides of cliffs, and massive rivers surged over the banks.

Thanks to the rain, Kate was unable to come over at all. The only time I saw her was on the school bus and at lunch. Our school bus had actually gotten stuck twice because of the mud and rain. And just yesterday, the road leading from the

mountains into Kingsplot had washed out. There was no longer any way for us to get to town. It was nice to have a break
from school, but it also meant no Kate and no Wyatt and no
fun.

I braved the rain once to go visit Kate, but it took me almost an hour and a half to trudge over the mushy, muddy
ground. Plus, when I made it to her house, her mom and dad
were both there, and Kate couldn't use the excuse that she was
going for a walk to get out. So I had to hike back, which took
about two hours.

As difficult as it was to get to Kate's, it was even more of a
challenge to visit the cave. The forest was like a swamp and the
water running down the stone stairway was so constant that
moving up each stair was a major accomplishment. I had gotten up there only twice to check on the stone. The leafy cocoon
was huge and throbbing when I last saw it. I figured I'd look in
on it again once the clouds stopped ruining everything.

So for the most part I just stayed indoors, searching the
manor for more hidden secrets and bugging Millie and Thomas
and Wane. I did spend a little time in the basement. It was
still buried, but the parts we had used previously were open.
I couldn't take the tunnels all the way to the conservatory because water had filled most of the passageway.

I did find a metal ladder hidden in a chimney of one of the

large fireplaces in the middle of the manor. It was a fireplace that we never used, and when I climbed up the ladder it ended in a closet just below the top floor. It was obvious that there were a number of ways to get around the manor. It made me both excited and nervous. I figured if I could get around, then so could anyone else.

The secret passages were cool, but I could only waste so much time in them. That meant I found myself spending way too much time just sitting in the kitchen willing the rain to stop and talking to Millie.

"This stinks," I said to Millie as I sat at the counter and nibbled at a piece of pie she had given me.

"That's the mold from all the rain," she replied.

I almost smiled. "I mean it stinks to be trapped indoors."

"Oh," she said, sniffing dryly and rolling out some more dough.

"Has it ever rained like this before?" I asked.

"It always rains," she informed me.

"I'm aware of that," I said. "But it doesn't always rain this hard."

"True, I can't remember such rain," she mused. "I hope your father's all right."

"Me too."

Millie cut the dough into circles and then placed them into pie tins. "Do you want to help me crimp them?" she asked.

I wanted nothing to do with crimping.

Wane came in and challenged me to a game of chess. I challenged her to find something less boring for me to do, and she failed. So, I halfheartedly played chess with her in one of the formal dining rooms. At first I could kind of tolerate it, but then it got so amazingly dull I felt forced to shake things up by spilling what I knew.

"Did you know that there are secret passages in this house?" I asked her.

"Check," she replied.

"You did?"

"No, *check,* as in your king's in trouble."

"Is the king the one with the cross on top?"

Wane nodded.

"So you don't know about the passages?" I asked again while moving my king to the left and out of immediate danger.

"I've discovered one or two passageways over the years as I have helped take care of this place," she replied. "This manor's full of surprises. I use a secret passageway to get up to the second floor."

"What passageway is that?" I asked.

"You enter it through the large kitchen cabinets where the brooms are," she whispered sounding secretive. "Check."

"Oh yeah, I gotcha," I winked.

"No," she laughed. "The check part was for the game again."

"Right," I waved, moving one of my little pieces to the opposite corner of the board.

"You can't do that," she laughed.

I moved my piece back and shifted my king. "Why didn't you tell me about the passageways?"

"It's not like you need more things to distract you," she answered.

"That's true, but doesn't that interest you, all the secret things here?"

Wane looked up from the board. "I learned years ago that this place is more amazing than I will ever know. Secret passages are great, but even greater things have happened here."

"Have you seen the slides?"

Wane appeared confused.

"There are slides in some of the secret passages," I explained.

She looked back at the chess board and shrugged. "Check."

I moved my castle to block her pointy guy. "Does my father know about the passageways?"

"I'm not sure what your father knows," she answered.

"Until you came along, it was always an unwritten rule that we not talk about these things."

"Is it written down now?" I joked.

"Check."

I sacrificed one of my horses. "I don't understand you," I said honestly. "You and Millie and Thomas and Scott move about this place like it's no big deal. Certainly all this stuff means something."

"It means it's distracted you enough to help me win—check."

I wanted to tell Wane about the cave and the new stone I had planted. I wanted to truly confide in her. But not only would she probably just say something like, "Been there, done that," but it just didn't feel right to inform her yet. I figured I would wait until I had done something really nice before I sprang it on her.

I took out one of her horses with my queen. "You haven't won yet."

Thunder shook the windows and rattled the chandelier above us.

"Have you ever seen it rain like this?" I asked.

"Never."

"Do you think something's askew?"

"Askew?" Wane asked.

"Cool word, huh? It means wrong."

She laughed. "I don't think anything's askew. But I think they'd better repair the washed-out road so you can go back to school."

"You don't enjoy my company?" I smiled.

"You know I do," she smiled back. "But how can you really appreciate someone if they're always around?"

I moved one of my castles, and she took it out with one of her short pieces.

"Why are you asking about the manor, Beck?" she questioned. "You're not planning anything we'll need to take out extra insurance for, are you?"

"Of course not," I said. "Check."

Wane looked at the board closely. "What do you mean check," she asked. "You can't get my king."

"You've been saying it," I complained. "I just wanted to say it too."

Wane shook her head.

"Who invented this game anyway?"

Wane started into some long, drawn-out story about the history of chess and how it was such a wonderful, brilliant game. She listed famous people and countries who revered it. I wanted to take my question back, but I thought that might be rude.

"Your turn," I said, hoping that would distract her from talking.

Wane moved her queen as the rain grew audibly louder.

"Don't you think we should build a boat or something?" I said nervously.

"Checkmate," was her only reply.

My sentiment exactly.

Illustration from page 31 of The Grim Knot

CHAPTER 15

The White Queen

I T'S HARD TO KEEP TRACK OF time when you have no school to go to and you're being held captive by Mother Nature in your own house. It also doesn't help when you can't see the sun. I wasn't completely sure what day it was anymore.

And still the rain kept coming.

Moments before I thought I was going to rip my ears off because of the constantly falling water, it stopped. Two days after it stopped, the clouds moved out, and a marvelous sun began to dry up the mess its nemesis had made.

Knowing Kate's parents still didn't want me talking to her, I called her up using star sixty-seven to hide my number on their caller ID. I pretended I was a girl from school named Jessica.

It was sort of embarrassing that her parents believed me so easily.

Having no school to attend and nothing but time on our hands, we made plans to meet behind the garage and check on our stone. I put on a sweatshirt and went to wait for her. It wasn't long before she showed up.

"Hi," I said coolly, as she came around the garage house corner.

I know it's not really great for my street credibility to admit this, but every time I saw Kate, things inside my stomach sort of jumped around, and my hands got sweaty. I mean, she was attractive, and I was heavily in *like* with her.

Kate hugged me and then asked where I had gotten such an ugly sweatshirt. I would have felt bad, but she was right. Thomas had bought the sweatshirt for me a couple of weeks before. It was yellow with light blue streaks across the top and a violin on it.

"Thomas bought it for me," I explained. "Every day he asks me when I'm going to wear it."

"I feel really lucky that today's the day," Kate smiled.

"He thinks I play the violin," I told her.

"Why does he think that?" she asked.

"Because I told him once that I needed to go practice the violin," I said. "I wanted to avoid cleaning a bunch of jars Millie needed for canning."

"Serves you right then," Kate said, staring at the sweatshirt.

We walked through the still-damp forest filling each other in on the boring things we had done since we last saw one another. When we reached the base of the mountain where the tracks and stairs went up, we had pretty much caught up on each other's life.

"I didn't miss these stairs," I said as we climbed.

"Me neither."

After we had hiked up and were inside the cave, I flipped the lights on. I wasn't surprised to find that everything was just as it was when I last left it. The large steel door leading into the massive cavern where the stone had been planted was still closed. I had shut it to make sure that nothing got in or out.

I ran to the big door and lifted the latch up. The larger cavern was lit, and I could see the four posts in the center of it. The huge, leafy cocoon was lying on the ground, split open.

"Kate!" I yelled.

"I'm right behind you," she whispered back.

"The dragon's gone."

"I can see that," she replied.

"Where is she?" I looked behind a tall pile of crates but she wasn't there. "How big do you think she is?"

"The others weren't too small," Kate answered while heading to the back tunnel door to make sure it was still locked.

I jumped onto one of the many barrels and glanced down.

I couldn't see anything other than crates, barrels, and poorly lit dirt. The large cage that was carved into the wall was empty as usual. I looked down into the small spring, but there was nothing in the water.

"The back door's still locked!" Kate shouted.

"Is she in a box?" I asked. "Did she dig down into the dirt? Wait, what about those crates?"

I ran to the far side and searched behind a wall of boxes that were too high to see behind. It was the last place she could possibly be, and I was fully expecting to see her crouched down hiding behind them.

There was nothing but shadows.

Both Kate and I walked back to the center of the massive cavern, figuratively scratching our heads. I looked down at the split cocoon. There was an imprint in the large cocoon, and thick yellow goo ran out of it.

"How could she get out of here?" I asked.

"What about your father?"

"I told him about the cave, but he wouldn't take . . . I mean why would he . . . I guess he could have," I moaned.

"Does your book say anything about what a queen dragon does once she's born?"

"I can't remember."

"That was a problem last time as well," Kate complained. "You've got to read."

"How about I give it to you and you read it?"

"That's not how it works," Kate reminded me.

"I can't believe she's gone."

I put my hands over my face and sighed heavenward. When I took my hands off my eyes, my head was tilted back, and something flashed briefly from the high ceiling of the cavern. I stepped back.

"Um, Kate," I whispered.

"What?"

"Look up."

Kate craned her head back and looked toward the ceiling. There was nothing but darkness there.

"Why am I doing this?" she asked.

"I thought I . . ."

Two eyes suddenly looked down at us. Kate actually screamed, and I gasped in air the wrong way and began to hiccup.

The eyes disappeared.

I know we had been trying to find her, but for some reason both of us turned and ran away. We actually had a pretty good reason. There was a dragon hanging over us on the ceiling. We crouched behind two empty barrels and whispered rapidly.

"Did you see that?" I hiccupped.

"No," Kate sassed back. "I just screamed for the fun of it."

"What do we do?"

"I have no idea."

We both stared up at the ceiling, looking for another sign of the dragon. There was some movement in the darkness, and a bit of white dropped from the black and then disappeared back up.

A huge hiccup sprang from my mouth. "Sorry," I said embarrassed. "I think that was part of her tail."

"All I saw was something white."

"We should get her some food," I suggested. "Maybe she'll come down for that."

"We're going to carry food up those stairs?" Kate whined. "That'll be awful."

"We could get the train working," I suggested again. Sure it was a hundred years old, and, yes, there was a forest growing over its tracks. But I remember some adult once saying something like, 'trying is good.' And even though it was an adult who said it, it still seemed like half-decent advice—at least in the case of trying to get a cool, old train running.

"That train's never going to run," Kate insisted.

"I'm just suggesting we try," I argued. "If we can't . . ."

I stopped talking because a loud screech shot through the cavern and echoed off the walls like a zillion fiery Ping-Pong balls. Both Kate and I jumped.

"She doesn't sound friendly," Kate whispered as we hid behind the barrels.

"What does friendly sound like?" I asked. "Did you expect her to giggle?"

Kate elbowed me hard.

"You know there's that cereal stuff in those barrels," I reminded her, pointing to the other side of the cavern. "That dog-food-looking junk. Maybe she'll eat that."

"That's not edible," Kate said.

"Wyatt tried some."

"I've got to start hanging out with other people," Kate griped.

"That's probably good advice," I agreed, followed by a big hiccup. "I hope you don't follow it."

Kate actually smiled.

"I'll tell you what," I said, pumped up by how pretty she was when she smiled. "I'll run across the cave and get some."

"Great," Kate said, no longer smiling. "But are you sure we actually want her to come down?"

"I'm not that terribly sure of anything," I reminded her.

I jumped up and ran closer to the wall. Then I moved along the edge of the cavern and worked my way over to the far side. When I got to the barrels, I unlatched one of the large wooden lids and took out a handful of the stuff. I looked across the cavern at Kate. She was staring at the ceiling with her mouth agape. I glanced up to see what she was looking at.

"Watch out, Beck!" she screamed.

As I looked up, a huge white flash bowled me over backward. I fell on the dirt. The cereal stuff I had been holding flew all over, covering me with a torrent of grain.

I looked up, and the dragon was perched on the edge of the barrel, eating straight from the barrel and taking bites bigger than anyone with good manners should.

I crab-walked backward, staring at her. She was already about the size of a large dog—stark white with cobalt blue talons and eyes. Her scales wrapped around her body in a circular pattern and her folded wings looked wet and rubbery. She had two small horns on her head that angled back and in. When she turned to gaze at me her horns looked sort of like a half halo. Her tail was long and the end was so thin she could coil it, which she did repeatedly as she ate. Her teeth were already impressive, and she had round bumps on her back. All four of her legs were muscular, and there were feathers around her wrists and ankles. There was something about her that made her different from the other dragons I had raised. She looked confident and majestic, and she was probably the coolest thing I had ever laid eyes on.

I hiccupped loudly.

The dragon looked at me. Her nostrils flared, and I could

see food sliding down her throat. She belched, and bits of dusty grain drifted down on me.

"Kate!" I whispered loudly.

"I'm right behind you," she replied. She had moved across the room and was now standing next to me.

The queen continued to stare at me. She then opened her wings as wide as she could and stood up on the rim of the barrel.

"Should we run?" I asked.

Kate was speechless.

The dragon folded her wings back in and then jumped softly down to the dirt. She sniffed and blinked her blue eyes twice. The only thing I could think of was to talk to her.

"Hello."

The dragon sniffed and shifted and then pawed at the ground gently.

"I'm Beck and this is Kate," I explained.

"She doesn't speak English," Kate said.

"Well, it's not like I speak dragon," I replied, turning my head to see Kate. "What else can I do? It's not like I know . . ."

I heard a snort and felt hot breath on the side of my face. I turned. The dragon was just inches away from me, standing on her two back legs. She sniffed the air directly beneath my chin and then dropped back down onto all fours.

Her eyes were intoxicatingly blue, and the scales on her face sparkled like diamonds. I reached out and touched the top of her nose. She tipped her head up as if encouraging me to continue. I patted her head and ran my hand over her left ear. She sniffed again and moved closer. So I put my right arm around her neck and bent down.

"Are you hugging her?" Kate asked.

"I'm not sure," I said awkwardly.

Kate stepped over to the barrel and got a big handful of the cereal. She came back and held the food out for the queen.

"Here you go," she offered.

The dragon ate it while Kate petted her and I continued to awkwardly hug her.

"She's beautiful," Kate said breathlessly.

"Different than the others, isn't she?"

Kate nodded.

"She kinda glows," I added.

"What about a name?" Kate questioned. "It has to be a nice one, seeing how that old guy told you she was a queen."

"Well, what's that one famous queen's name, Queen Ellen or something?"

"Queen Ellen?" Kate laughed. "You mean Queen Elizabeth?"

"Maybe," I said with a hiccup.

"You wanna name her Elizabeth?" Kate asked.

"No, that's too long," I said, angry that my hiccups hadn't ceased. "How about Lizzy? Like Lizzy Stephens."

"Who's that?"

"She was a girl with big feet in my third grade class."

Kate tried it out. "What do you think, Lizzy?" she said kindly. "Are you okay with that name?"

Lizzy tilted her head up as if she were beginning to nod but stopped in the middle of it.

"Half a nod's not bad," I said.

"I agree," Kate smiled.

We spent the rest of the afternoon petting and feeding Lizzy. We kept making up excuses to stay longer.

"We haven't brushed her ankles yet."

"I think we need to count her scales."

Eventually Kate had to get home. I offered to stay with Lizzy, but Kate looked mad that I would stay when she had to leave. We said good-bye, closed and locked the rolling steel door, and left through the moss.

It was really painful; neither of us had any desire to leave. We talked about nothing but Lizzy until we reached the garage house and had to split up.

I said good-bye to Kate with a giant hiccup.

Illustration from page 33 of The Grim Knot

CHAPTER 16

She Makes Me

I COULDN'T THINK ABOUT ANYTHING else besides Lizzy. It was like my brain had gone haywire. When I got back to the manor Millie made me a great dinner, but I couldn't taste it. My senses were all focused on Lizzy. When Thomas sat me down for half an hour and gave me a lecture on how I needed to practice the violin more often, I couldn't even hear him enough to be bothered. My brain was too preoccupied with Lizzy. And when Wane came up to my room and asked if I wanted to play a game of chess, my only reply was, "Lizzy."

Wane looked at me like I had gone insane and then shut my door and left. I don't know what my problem was. It was as if the white dragon had cast a spell over me.

I fell asleep mumbling her name and when I woke up it was the first word I said.

"Lizzy."

I jumped out of bed looking for my clothes. Thunder cracked and rattled my window violently. I turned to witness the downpour outside.

"No!" I moaned.

My window looked like the backside of a waterfall.

"Come on," I complained. "Enough already with the rain."

When I got down to the kitchen, Millie was wearing galoshes and a rain bonnet. She was sitting on a stool wringing her hands and listening to the radio. The announcer was talking about more washed-out roads.

"Are you okay?" I asked.

"I'm worried," she replied. "What if the roads don't get fixed? We need to get into town. I'm running low on essentials. I only have fifty more pounds of flour."

"Oh," I shrugged. "I thought you were worried about my father."

"That too," she admitted.

"It's raining harder than before," I groused.

"I don't know what's happening," Millie said. "Thomas said bits of our drive are beginning to wash away and part of the stone fence near the gate has collapsed. The soil is just so saturated."

Despite her condition, Millie made me some perfectly scrambled eggs with thick delicious gravy and pull-apart butter biscuits. There was also a plate full of thick maple bacon and crispy golden hash browns.

"You're going to make me fat," I told her.

"Thanks, Beck," she said kindly.

I finished my breakfast and then stood at the door watching the clouds vomit huge amounts of water down upon everything. The courtyard had at least a foot of standing water in it and the snake statue was overflowing. I could see scattered tree branches that had been knocked down by the wind and rain.

Lightning flashed, temporarily blinding my eyes. Thunder followed right behind it, scorching my ears. Everything I could see shouted, "Don't go out." But I knew there was no way I was going to stay away from that cave.

I went up to my room and changed into my boots and old jeans. I pulled out a plastic windbreaker that Thomas had purchased for me. I had made a personal decision never to wear it, but now things had changed.

I threw the windbreaker on and zipped it up. I put on a ball cap and then put one on top of that, backwards so that I had a brim in front and in back. I thought it was such a great idea that I put two more on top of those so that I had a brim on all four sides. I looked in the mirror and shuddered—I looked beyond dorky. There was no way I would ever go out like this if I knew I would see people.

I knew that Millie would be expecting me to come down for lunch, so I devised a plan to throw her off. I returned to the kitchen and began packing a lunch.

"What are you doing?" Millie asked.

"Packing a lunch. I'm going to pretend like I'm camping in the manor," I lied.

"Well, that sounds like fun," she said. "What are you wearing though?"

I looked down at my windbreaker. "It's my safari outfit."

"What an imagination you have," she said sweetly. I was a little offended that Millie thought I was the kind of teenager who would dress up and have pretend safaris. But she followed up her remarks by packing me two sandwiches, a container of potato salad, a banana, what looked like half a chocolate cake, and a thermos of hot apple cider. She wrapped everything up in butcher paper and put it in a big brown bag.

I thanked her and left the kitchen. I walked to one of the back doors on the north wing, put my huge lunch bag beneath my arm, and moved out into the deluge.

I was instantly soaked.

By the time I made it over behind the garage, my lunch bag had completely dissolved as well as the paper covering my food. All I had was a big armful of mush and a wet banana. I dropped the food and watched it smoosh into the flood of water.

The ground behind the garage was so soggy it was almost impossible to walk on. I could see the train tracks running right into the wall. The water had washed away most of the soil around it, exposing about ten feet of the track going into the woods. I walked along the track as much as I could. Some sections of the rails were still slightly buried, but there were also long stretches where the whole track, or at least the metal rails, were totally visible. I balanced myself on the rails, making better time than I thought I would.

The rain was still coming down in pool-sized drops, but there was some protection from the trees. All over the forest I could see and hear rushing rainwater. I made the mistake of stepping off the track once, and my legs sunk about a foot into mud. It took me five minutes to pull myself out and another ten minutes to dig out my right shoe that had been sucked off.

The rain wasn't too cold, but the wind blowing on my wet body made me shiver violently. I pushed on, feeling like a post-man in a storm. Normally I would have given up, but I kept thinking about Lizzy—she was like a magnet pulling me toward her.

When I reached the side of the mountain, water was flowing rapidly down the stone stairs, and the bush near the entrance had been washed away.

I traveled on.

My clothes were so wet it felt like I was lifting an extra

hundred pounds with each step. My dorky-looking hats did a pretty good job of keeping the rain out of my eyes, but did nothing for all the water that was flowing down the front and back of my neck. Once it flowed down into my shirt and jacket, there was no stopping it from running down into my pants.

I could feel a great chafing coming on.

I didn't have a watch, and of course there was no sun to help me gauge the time. But it felt like forever before I reached the moss wall. Water ran down from above and then diverged when it reached the thick moss and flowed past each side. I expected the cave to be really wet, but there were only some small puddles right by the entrance.

I stepped in further and looked at the massive train. I wished so badly it worked so I could drive it back to the manor.

When I rolled open the large steel door, Lizzy was hanging from the ceiling by her back legs and her wings were wrapped around her like a cocoon. She looked considerably bigger than yesterday, but I figured my eyes were just playing tricks.

She screeched and dropped from the ceiling, landing on all fours. She walked majestically toward me. I could feel my chest pounding and my limbs were buzzing. Her blue eyes looked directly at me as she swaggered.

She stopped right in front of me and snorted.

It wasn't hard to notice that her head was now higher than

mine. She had gone from the size of a large dog to the size of a large horse. She lowered her noggin and nudged my right hand. I scratched her behind the ear.

"What happened?" I asked.

She raised her tail and swatted it down against the ground.

"You're huge," I said. "No offense, but, I mean, look at you!"

Lizzy grumbled, and I scratched harder. I looked around the cavern and saw that three of the barrels had been knocked over and were broken open.

"So, you just ate the whole time I was gone?"

She opened her mouth, and I could see her long purple tongue. It flicked out and then curled back in. Like the rest of her, her teeth had increased in size. I made a mental note never to stick my hand in her mouth.

Lizzy lifted her head and nudged me under the chin.

"You're like a big dog," I told her while patting her on the side of her long neck. "Making me pet you—the other dragons never did that. Of course, they didn't grow as fast either."

Lizzy strode over to the spring and took a long drink. I walked to the center of the cavern and looked at her split-open pod. I could see that she had made some sort of nest in the dirt next to the cocoon. I sat down cross-legged and watched her drink. She was mesmerizing to observe. Everything about her was breathtaking.

Lizzy finished drinking and turned around. She stepped closer and then stopped. I patted the ground thinking it might make her come.

"Come," I called.

Lizzy looked at me and then suddenly sprang up toward the ceiling. Her body twisted, and she was lost in the dark shadows of the pockmarked ceiling.

"Wow," I whispered.

I moved over so that I was directly under her and lay down on the dirt. I put my arms behind my head and gazed up. I couldn't see her, but I knew she was there. She opened her eyes and blinked.

"Yeah, I see you."

I could hear her breathing. The only other sound was coming from the spring as it gurgled. Lizzy snorted and spit dropped down on my face.

"Thanks," I said, scooting over a bit.

It was sort of pleasant lying there—the sound of Lizzy breathing up above and the cool dirt against my wet back. Sure I had mud all over me and two of my hats had been knocked off. And yes, my legs burned and my teeth were chattering, but for some reason as I lay there I couldn't remember ever feeling more at peace.

"What's the deal with you?" I asked Lizzy as I stared up into the dark.

I closed my eyes and wished my lunch hadn't been destroyed by the rain. Luckily I was so relaxed it didn't really bother me. I was completely at ease until I heard a knock.

My eyes sprang open.

I wanted to pretend the noise away, but I heard it again. It was a hollow rapping sound and it was coming from the direction of the tunnel door.

"Can moths knock?" I asked Lizzy.

She didn't reply.

There was another knock, followed by the muffled sound of someone shouting. My cold body shivered and shook. I looked toward the steel door on the other side of the cavern. Most of me wanted to just get up and run out of it and out of the cave. But a tiny bit of me was worried that whatever was knocking was in trouble and needed help. Maybe moths were attacking it–them–whatever.

The knocking grew louder and more urgent.

I wish I had been a Boy Scout longer. I might have learned how to deal with these kinds of things. After all, it had all the classic Boy Scout elements: a cave, someone yelling for help, my stomach was tied in a square knot, plus I was a boy.

I stood up not sure which direction to go.

Illustration from page 38 of The Grim Knot

CHAPTER 17

Liar

I WAS THINKING I HAD PICKED the wrong direction as I ran toward the tunnel door. I couldn't help it; what if it were Kate or my dad knocking?

The pounding was loud and frantic. I stood in front of the tunnel door and listened. I could hear hollering, but I couldn't make out what was being said.

"Who's there?" I yelled back.

The pounding and the hollering continued.

"Who is it?" I yelled louder.

The pounding stopped for a moment and then started up again. The volume of the hollering increased. I could barely make out one of the words being screamed:

"Please!"

I hesitated for a moment, but since they were polite enough to scream "Please," I figured they couldn't be all bad.

I flipped the back switch down, and the lights went out. If there were moths in there, I didn't want them swarming out as I unlocked the door. It was very dark now. A tiny bit of gray was seeping in from the open steel door but it was barely enough to let me see anything.

I held my arms out and reached for the tunnel door. I grabbed the large metal latch in my hands.

"It's not like I haven't done stupid stuff before," I rationalized.

I lifted the latch up, and the door quickly began to push out. I reached to grab the doorknob, but I was blocked by a large body stumbling toward me. I couldn't tell if I was being attacked or if they were just falling. If it was an attacker, they were one of the worst assailants ever. They groaned, and I could tell it was a man. He went limp, and the weight of his body falling toward mine pushed us both to the ground.

I rolled out from under him.

The man lay motionless on the ground, the skin on his hands glowing.

"Whitey," I whispered.

My pale visitor groaned. I stood up, shut the door, and switched the lights back on. I looked over to where Lizzy was hanging, but I couldn't see her. The lighting was so bad in the cavern it was hard to clearly see anything more than a few feet way. I looked down at Whitey. His face was hidden by his robe, but his mouth was visible and panting.

"What were you doing back there?" I asked.

He coughed and sputtered for a moment and then spoke. "I was coming up from the far caves. I didn't expect the tunnel door to be locked."

"Was anybody chasing you?"

He shook his head.

"Did you see any moths?"

"No."

"So why were you knocking and screaming?"

"I am exhausted," he said. "My body is weak, and I knew if I didn't get out, I might not make it all the way through the long tunnel."

I looked closely at him. He was wearing the same brown robe with orange circles around the sleeve. His lips were still white and cakey. His skin looked so dry I could see the cracks in it.

"You found the cave," he said breathing hard, his high voice almost piercing.

I nodded. "So what is this place?"

"I believe your great-grandfather found it," he said softly.

"He discovered that this particular mountain was full of caves and tunnels, and he figured it would be a fantastic attraction for the family. He had the stone stairs carved out, but what he really wanted was something mechanical to bring him up. He thought about a tram or a gondola, but what he really wanted was a train. So he . . ."

Whitey took a moment to calm his breathing.

"And?" I asked impatiently.

"Someone said that it was impossible because the mountain is so steep. But that just made your great-grandfather more determined to figure it out—which he did. He created a train that could bend up and down so it could ride on a track as steep as this mountain. Of course train wheels aren't designed to climb, so he put in the cable. It could pull the train up as well as help it descend slowly."

"Does it still work?"

"The engine hasn't been stoked for years. Your great-grandfather ran the track from here to the garage house where it goes underground and stops below the basement of the manor."

"Wow."

"But there was a problem," Whitey coughed. "An accident. While the train was bending to enter the cave, a dear relative was caught between the two shifting segments and died. Your great-grandfather was devastated. He parked the train up here, buried the tracks, and cemented the back of the garage house where it had once entered. He never set foot in here again."

"So, does it still work?" His story was sad and all that, but I guess I had a one-track mind.

"It might," he said, flustered. "But it has nowhere to go. That's not the point. The point is that you found the cave. Did you find the stone?"

I honestly didn't know how much to tell this guy. He was more than creepy, but I had a feeling he was somehow connected to my family.

"Who are you?" I asked.

"That's not important," he replied.

"It is if you want to know about the stone."

"My name is Hagen," he said reluctantly. "Sergio Hagen."

"Hagen like the valley?" I asked.

He nodded. "Did you find the stone?"

"Maybe," I answered.

"And you planted it?"

"I set it here on the dirt," I explained. "And it's growing."

"You Pillages and your gift—simply amazing. Now you must kill it as soon as it's born."

"What?" I asked, even though I remembered clearly that he

had already told me to do that. I think I just pushed it aside thinking he was crazy. "Why?"

"You must kill it," he reiterated. "*The Grim Knot* should have explained it all."

"That book doesn't say anything about killing a queen dragon," I argued.

"If she ages it'll be too late," he panicked.

"I thought you said it would only be too late if I didn't plant the stone in time."

"That was a lie," he admitted. "I simply needed you to move quickly."

"What?" I asked, bothered by his deceit. "So I didn't have to plant it?"

"It has to end."

"What has to end?"

"As long as that stone was around, your family would never be well," he whispered harshly. "Even if you were to avoid the sickness and obsession, the dragons would bring your children, or your children's children great misery."

"I don't have any kids," I pointed out.

"Time changes things like that," he said sadly. "You must kill her."

"What if I can't?" I asked. "What if I don't want to?"

"The book will tell you everything."

"I've read the book," I complained. "And to be honest with you, it's a little choppy. Why don't you just tell me what you know?"

"I only know what I've been told," he said solemnly. "And your father was promised that answers were hidden in the book."

"This is crazy," I growled. "I don't even know you, and I don't want to kill any more dragons."

Whitey stood up and faced the tunnel. "This is all wrong. Good-bye, Beck."

"What?" I questioned. "I thought you were too weak to make it back that way?"

"I lied," he said.

"You lied about the seven days," I said angrily. "And you lied about this. How can I believe anything you say?"

"The book," he said with authority. "You have done well to plant the stone, but now you must finish it."

"But . . ."

"Finish what you started," he snapped.

I stood there and watched him go back into the tunnel. He turned around and told me to lock the door behind him. I had never been a big fan of being told what to do, but I kind of liked the idea of Whitey being trapped in a tunnel.

I shut the door and slipped the metal latch back into place.

I stayed around for another hour staring up at the ceiling, but Lizzy never came down.

When I left, it was raining harder than ever. I made it down the stairs, and, as I walked home through the forest, I saw that more of the track was washed off.

I was mad as I walked along the old, wet railroad ties. I was mad that it was raining so hard, mad that my father had abandoned me, mad that I had to leave Lizzy, and mad that all the answers to my questions were not just being handed to me. If I were more mature, I'd probably just say something like "Where's the fun in that?" But I wasn't more mature and, at the moment, things felt less than fun.

Illustration from page 40 of The Grim Knot

CHAPTER 18

Is This the World They Created?

I'LL BE HONEST, I'M NOT ONE OF those people who loves antiques and collectables. I don't even want to think about having to go antiquing—in fact, I'm kind of uncomfortable just saying the word. Sometimes I have a hard time around older people. I don't like old movies, old music, or old stories. I like new cars and new movies and new music. I love the manor, but I also love Xboxes and TVs and multiple phones. Once when my mother, Francine, was still alive and she was in one of her rare good moods, she took me on a trip to a nearby ghost town. It was okay, I guess. There was a saloon and actors walking around doing tricks with guns. There was also a photography store where people could dress up in old western wear and have their picture taken. My mom wanted a picture of the two of us so badly that I had to give in. I refused to wear the old clothes, however. So the picture was of my mom dressed like a saloon girl on a stagecoach and me standing next to her in a Halo T-shirt and sneakers.

I just don't get excited about most old things.

The Grim Knot was an exception. It was a very old book, but for some reason I really liked it. I had found it in one of the cleared-out tunnels in the basement. Milo had planted it there so that I would read it and unknowingly help him raise the dragons. The book had helped; it had clued me in on what I had to do and had caused me to accuse Kate of being the evil-doer instead of Milo. Luckily, Kate turned out to be non-evil and Milo was gone for good.

I liked to just look at the book. I wasn't too hyped about reading it again, but I didn't mind looking at it. I had read it all the way through once, and I really thought that was enough. I can hardly sit through a movie twice, much less read a book a second time. But as I lay on my bed, listening to the rain beat up the manor, and holding the book in my hands, it occurred to me that perhaps the solution to me not having to kill Lizzy was in there. I needed to grow up and do my part. So, I carefully flipped through the book reading certain sections over and looking closely for any small handwritten notes or hidden clues. I did find a tiny sentence written under the edge of the back cover. It read: "Is this the world we have created?"

I wished all my dead ancestors had cell phones. It would be so much easier to just call them up, ask them a few questions, and be done with it. It was a dumb wish. Besides, for all I knew, maybe they did have cell phones, but they couldn't reach me because *I* didn't. I made a mental note to try that argument with my father when he returned. I really wanted a cell phone.

A storm-broken branch slammed up against my window followed by the flash of lightning. Luckily the glass didn't break. I should have been worried, but my attention was with *The Grim Knot.*

As I read the excerpts that so many of my ancestors had written, my mind began to race. I could see the Isle of Man in the middle of the Irish Sea where those people had once lived. I could see the fields of grain they grew under the influence of our family gift. And I could see stones and dragons and feel the greed and power and uncontrollable obsession. The world my ancestors had created became almost real to me.

I saw time slowing to the point where it was now, and where I was left to make what seemed like monumental decisions.

"This stinks," I moaned.

I couldn't see anything in *The Grim Knot* that offered me answers to the problems I was now facing.

I held the book up and pulled the covers open letting the pages hang down over me as I laid in my bed. I shook it thinking that maybe something would fall out.

Nothing besides disappointment drifted down on me.

I rolled over and placed the book on my pillow. Mr. Binkers had fallen off my dresser and was laying on the floor facedown. I stuck my leg out and flipped him over with my foot.

"Maybe if I close my eyes," I told him.

I shut my eyes and felt the front of the cover. Bits of it were raised, but they didn't mean anything. I felt the inside pages for some secret bumps or braille markings. The only thing I felt besides stumped was a small bit of dried chocolate that my fingers had accidentally smeared on page thirty-three.

Rain beat like a tommy gun against my window.

I turned to the back cover and re-read the tiny words that had been hidden under the loose leather edge. I tried to read some hidden meaning into it, but I couldn't think of anything plausible.

I pulled at the loose leather, and it tore away from the edge a little more.

"Oops," I said, trying to press it back.

It wouldn't stay folded over the edge so I licked my index finger and moistened the edge where it had been glued down. I'm not completely sure what I thought that would accomplish.

I guess I was thinking that it would moisten the old glue residue and hold the edge down. It didn't and, in fact, the little bit of water I had smeared on the edge caused the leather to peel back even further. I was considering using chewing gum to hold it in place when I noticed something. Right where the leather was coming off was the tiniest bit of white. I thought it was just a flaw in the leather or a scratch, but when I examined it closer I could see it wasn't either of those things. Now instead of trying to fix the book, I pulled the leather away from the back cover. I made about a two-inch gap between the stiff book board and the leather that had been glued to it.

I looked into the gap and gaped.

There was a small piece of white paper. It had been sealed up between the back of the book and the leather that was wrapped over it. I carefully tugged the tiny paper out. It was about the size of a business card and had one corner missing. There were some big numbers scribbled on one side and on the other side was a list written in really tiny handwriting. It looked like a column of names with numbers after each one.

Thunder cracked, making the discovery feel almost sinister.

I held the card close to my eyes as I examined every centimeter of it. I carefully tore off more of the back cover to see if there was anything else hidden. There wasn't. I peeled off the edging of the front cover and checked under it.

There was nothing but book.

I looked at the big scribbled numbers on the front of the card again and wished that Kate were with me. She was so much better with numbers and math. It was difficult to even read the list of words on the back because of their size, but I did make out the first word.

"Hunched."

The word was followed by the number 1. I'd like to think that if I hadn't been so tired from traveling to the cave, or so confused about what to do, that I would have figured it out instantly. But it wasn't until almost a half hour later, while looking through the book for the fiftieth time, that I noticed the illustration on page one was of a dragon hunching.

My room lit up from a flash of nearby lightning. I counted to two and thunder shook the windows and vibrated through my chest.

I looked at the card again. I couldn't make out the second word on the list, but I could decipher the number after it: 70.

I turned to page seventy. It was one of the last pages in the book and there was a drawing of a dragon with its wings spread. I checked the card and with the help of the picture could make out the small word.

"Wingspan."

I quickly worked through the rest of the book. All of the

numbers after the words corresponded to illustrations in the book. And all the words were descriptions of what the dragon in the illustration was doing—sleeping, attacking, flying, etc . . . I was pretty excited about figuring it out, but also disappointed that it didn't seem to mean anything.

"What good is that?" I complained to Mr. Binkers.

I looked at the ten scribbled numbers on the other side of the card—27, 1, 20, 8, 70, 9, 54, 6, 40. I realized the random numbers were no longer completely random, they all were numbers of pages with illustrations on them. It made sense that the order that the numbers were written in was important, so I wrote down the title of the pictures in the order of the numbers, thinking it would make a sentence that would tell me some great secret.

"Flying, hunched, drinking, attack, wingspan, sleeping, clawing, screeching, dead—it all makes perfect sense now," I said sarcastically to myself.

I checked out the illustrations four more times and was about to just throw the book across the room and call it quits when I finally saw what I needed to see.

"Yes!"

I knew all my days of looking at *I Spy* books and reading *Where's Waldo* would pay off. I was pretty happy to have figured it out and felt slightly smug in the knowledge that I had always known pictures really were the best part of a book.

I stayed awake long into the night, listening to the rain and staring intently at pictures of dragons.

Illustration from page 42 of The Grim Knot

CHAPTER 19

Misfire

THUNDER RUDELY WOKE ME up at eight in the morning. I grumbled at Mother Nature and tried to go back to sleep. But the thunder was like an alarm that went off every few seconds, and unfortunately, the weather didn't have a snooze button.

I sat up in bed and yawned.

The Grim Knot was resting on my dresser next to Mr. Binkers. What I learned from it last night didn't make me feel any better. In fact it scared me even more. I was so happy to discover what was hidden, but I wished it had been a different finding.

I got up, dressed, and threw on my windbreaker. Last night while taking my windbreaker off, I had found a thin plastic zipper around the back of the collar. When I unzipped it, an attached hood came out. It was way easier to just use the hood instead of baseball caps.

I ran down to the kitchen to use the only phone in the manor. Of course Millie was there, and she was peeling carrots.

"I wish we had another phone," I complained.

"We have one," Millie pointed.

"I know that," I told her. "I just wish we had one with a little more privacy—or maybe a cordless one."

"I like a cord on my phone," Millie insisted. "It's more stable."

Millie stopped peeling carrots and started to mix something in a large orange bowl. It didn't look like she was going to step out of the kitchen to give me any privacy. I glanced out one of the many kitchen windows that the wind was shoving raindrops against and shrugged. I picked up the phone and dialed star sixty-seven followed by Kate's number. It rang four times before her father answered.

"Yes, sir, this is Timothy. I am a student in one of Kate's classes," I said while pinching my nose. I didn't actually enjoy lying, but I needed to talk to Kate. "I live in town, and I know she can't get to school. I thought I'd tell her what we've been learning."

Kate's dad commented on how thoughtful I was while

Millie just stared at me. Seventeen seconds later Kate greeted me on the other line."

"Hello, Timothy."

"Hi," I said, knowing she knew it was me. I needed to tell her what happened yesterday, but I didn't want Millie to hear. "So you know that girl, Lizzy, in your zoology class?" I asked.

"Yes," Kate played along.

"Well, she's huge."

Millie slapped me with a dish towel.

"That's not a bad thing," I said to Kate, trying not to sound so harsh. "It's just an observation. Oh, and that really old white dress you like . . ."

"Yes . . ." Kate said slowly.

"Well, I saw it . . . in a magazine ad," I told her.

"When did you go to the cave?" Kate asked, obviously not in the same room as her parents.

"A couple of times."

"And that old guy was there?"

I nodded, realized she couldn't see me do so, and said, "Yes. That white dress came out of the back room."

Millie looked at me and raised her eyebrows as high as she could.

"Can you get over here so we can study?" I asked Kate.

"Have you seen the rain?"

"Is it raining?" I asked as thunder simultaneously ripped through the air.

"I'm not a big fan of being struck by lightning," she said.

"Just duck as you walk."

"I'll try," she said, laughing. "If I'm not there in two hours, I've given up."

"That's the spirit."

"Bye, Beck."

"Bye, Kate."

I hung up the phone. Millie was staring at me with her good eye and both eyebrows arched.

"That was an unusual call," she observed. "You're not up to something, are you?"

I shook my head.

"Kate's a smart girl," she said, wagging her finger. "But I don't want you hurting her. You should know that just because your father isn't around doesn't give you permission to run around all willy-nilly."

"Willy who?" I asked.

"Beck, this weather can be very dangerous," she lectured. "Combine that with your personality and . . ." Millie cut her sentence short and shivered as if there had been a disturbance in the force.

I looked out the window and halfway changed the subject. "When do you think it is going to stop raining anyhow?"

"It does make one worry," she said. "Thomas is filling sand-bags out by the stables."

"That's great," I cheered, looking around for breakfast.

"He's thinking he might need to sandbag some areas. The water's getting dangerously close to the south end of the manor."

"Wow."

"He could use your help," she added.

"Really? Cause normally I'd be in school," I reminded her. "I mean I don't want him to count on me being around when that's not always possible."

Millie scowled at me, and her wrinkly face bunched up like a rapidly drying prune.

"I was just trying to think of others," I told her.

Millie opened the oven and pulled out a plate of food that had been warming. She handed me a huge biscuit with a thick slice of ham, a fried egg, and melted cheese in the middle of it. "Eat it fast and then go help Thomas before you have to study."

I shoved the biscuit sandwich into my mouth and took a huge bite. It was even better than it looked and smelled. Millie filled up a large glass with milk and pushed it over to me.

"You should cook for a king or something," I mumbled with a mouth full of ham and cheese. "Or Oprah."

"Oh, I don't think they'd want me underfoot," Millie blushed.

I couldn't imagine anyone who ate who wouldn't want Millie underfoot. I had a second sandwich, changed things up with a glass of fresh apple juice and then walked slowly down the mansion hallway toward the north end of the manor and in the general direction of the stables. As I stepped out one of the back doors and into the nonstop rain, I decided to at least walk behind the garage house and see if any more of the tracks were exposed.

They were. In fact they had been so cleared off by the rain, that they now looked completely unburied and almost usable.

I sloshed through the mud and slipped up between the garage house and the stables. I couldn't see Thomas, so I opened one of the large stable doors and entered. I followed the long dirt walkway between the stables—there were about fifteen on each side. At the far end was an open room with a hay-strewn floor and a round corral, and then two large barn doors opening to the outside. The doors were wide open and I could see a huge pile of sand. Thomas and Scott were shoveling at the base of it, filling sacks as fast as they could. Thomas was wearing nice trousers with large plastic boots. He had on a dress shirt with a vest over it, but he had gotten casual by rolling up his sleeves. Scott was in his usual grubby work attire.

I climbed over the corral fence and stepped up to Thomas.

"Millie said I should help," I informed him, hoping that by phrasing it like that he would tell me I didn't have to. He didn't fall for it.

"Excellent."

"I told her you probably don't want to get used to me helping because I'm usually in school."

"Grab a sack and start shoveling," Scott interrupted.

I figured Scott was just mad because I still blamed him for what I had done. I picked up a shovel and started pitching sand into a bag. We were under the lip of the roof outside the barn doors so the rain wasn't pelting us directly. But every time the wind blew east we got pretty wet. After about forty minutes, Scott left to check on some of the rain gutters. It struck me that since the tracks were exposed by nature, it couldn't hurt to ask about them.

"So, Thomas," I said.

"Yes," he replied.

"I was walking behind the garage to get here and there are some train tracks."

His shovel sliced into the mound of sand. "Really?"

"They run right into the back of the garage." I held a bag

open, and Thomas tossed sand into it. "The rain has washed away about a foot of soil. I guess they were buried."

"It's quite a wet spell," he said nonchalantly.

I tied up the bag and picked up an empty one. "So you didn't know about the train tracks?"

"I didn't say that," he answered, stopping to wipe his brow with a handkerchief. "There's a line of track that goes through the forest and up into the mountain."

"You don't say?" I said.

"I remember as a child playing in that forest," he replied. There was a faint smile on his lips. "The tracks were buried, but we found sections that were clean. All we ever found out was that your great-grandfather built the tracks as a beginning of what he hoped would be an elaborate mountain railroad."

"Wow." I mentally complimented myself on my great acting.

Thomas's shovel bit into the sandpile again. "There was an accident," he continued. "A boy was killed, and, like so many of your relatives do, they buried their problems. Years later your grandfather planted the trees that now cover the track. I remember being very curious as a child, but my mother said never to even ask about it."

It seemed weird to imagine Thomas having a mother.

"Well, the rain has washed the dirt away," I said as I picked up another full bag of sand and heaved it next to the others.

"I knew this weather was once in a lifetime," he said reflectively.

Scott came back and stopped our conversation. I was just about to fake an accident to get out of having to keep shoveling when Kate showed up. She came in through the stables and almost scared me to death when she crept up behind me and said, "Hello."

"Hello, Katherine," Thomas said nicely.

Scott just nodded. After my heart rate slowed, I informed Thomas and Scott that as much as I would have loved to stay and shovel, I needed to go and study with Kate. They took it pretty hard.

Kate and I walked back through the stables and over to the garage. When we reached the tracks we stopped to scrape mounds of mud off our boots. Kate was as wet as a person could be without actually drowning. Her hair was hanging from her head like cherry seaweed and the mascara around her blue eyes was running. She looked like a wet Goth angel. I commented on her appearance, and she started in on my windbreaker.

"What?" I said defensively. "It's the only thing I have that's rainproof."

"You gotta stop having Thomas shop for you," she smiled.

"He just shows up with these things. You should see some of the stuff I throw away."

"No, thanks," she said, trudging ahead of me along the rain-soaked tracks.

By the time we reached the cave we were so cold, tired, and drenched that my bones were soggy. I knew if I cracked my knuckles, water would spring out of my fingers. Despite our condition, the second I flipped on the lights I was excited. Apparently Kate felt likewise because she ran as fast as me to the large steel door.

We rolled it open and entered the massive back cavern.

"Lizzy!" I called out. "Lizzy!"

"I don't see her," Kate said frantically.

"Lizzy!"

All I saw were broken crates and split-open barrels that had once held dragon cereal. I could hear the sound of the spring gurgling and Kate breathing slowly. My eyes drifted back across the scene. The back door looked closed and the leafy cocoon was still lying in the center of the space next to its pole. Next to the cocoon were mounds of pushed-up dirt.

We both looked up at the ceiling.

"She's too big to completely hide in the darkness anymore," I told Kate. "Last time I saw her she was like a giant horse."

"Then where is she?"

"I don't know," I admitted. "But I'm sure she's bigger. Look at all the empty barrels."

"So she just ate herself into nonexistence?"

"Maybe she . . ." I didn't have to guess.

Loose dirt near the cocoon began to rumble up like the soil was giving birth. The ground shook, and Kate grabbed my right arm as the two of us stepped back. I could see something white rising.

Both Kate and I were struck speechless.

Lizzy continued to rise out of her dirt nest. She was mammoth; at least twice the size she had been when I last saw her. She pushed up on her legs and shook. Dirt flew around the cavern like terra-firma fireworks. A decent-sized clod smacked me in the face and stomach. Kate had the good sense to hide behind me.

Lizzy lifted her head and opened her wings. It looked as if she filled a fourth of the cavern. She folded her wings back, smacked her long white tail on the ground, and screeched. I could feel my eardrums melting. I put my hands over my ears and closed my eyes hoping that would help.

Lizzy stopped screaming, and I opened my eyelids.

Two very distinct thoughts were running through my mind. One, I had never seen anything so beautiful. I know a guy like me is not really supposed to be talking about beautiful, but that's what she was. I had seen ten other dragons before, and they were all amazing and awesome looking in their own right, but none of them looked like Lizzy. She appeared powerful just sitting there, and when she opened her wings she was no less spectacular than all eight wonders of the world. She made the pyramids look like baby blocks and the Great Wall of China seem like a hastily built backyard fence. I could barely breathe. My arms just hung to my sides and my body shivered—it felt like my fingernails were just going to slip off and drop into the dirt.

Lizzy lowered her head, and her blue eyes looked right through me.

The second thought running through my head was: I should have destroyed her the moment she was born. There was no way I could ever extinguish something so amazing and large.

Lizzy lowered her head to the ground in a submissive gesture. I could see that the horns above her ears were as long as elephant tusks now.

"She's unbelievable," Kate whispered. "My eyes aren't able to quite adjust."

"She wasn't this big yesterday," I whispered back.

"I think she wants you to climb on."

"What?" I asked. A thrill of excitement bounced around my body.

"Look at how she's standing."

Lizzy's head was resting on the ground, and her front legs were folded so that her shoulders were lowered.

"Maybe she wants you," I said, still whispering.

"You're the Pillage," Kate reminded me. "Get on."

"I should just walk up her neck?" I asked. "Like Fred Flintstone?"

Kate nodded.

I took little strides as I moved closer to Lizzy. Part of me wanted to cower in fear, but a larger part of me wanted to run toward her. I got about five feet away and stopped. She still hadn't moved. Her head was resting on the ground, and her eyes were looking up at me like a dog that was both loyal and nervous. She appeared even more dazzling up close. Her scales were like diamonds that circled around her entire body, and the feathers that were around her ankles flared out like flames. I could see a gray streak running over her ridged back and down her tail.

"Hey," I said soothingly. "Remember me?"

Lizzy snorted.

"I was here yesterday," I went on. "I helped you hatch." I looked back at Kate and she motioned for me to go on.

I took two steps closer.

"I'm not going to hurt you," I promised. "And hopefully you won't hurt me."

Two more steps.

I was close enough now that I could reach out and touch her. I shuffled my feet and got even nearer. I put my right hand out and touched her above the left eye. She felt like cool clay. Lizzy kept her head down and shivered. I watched the shiver move all the way down her back and shake out through the tip of her long tail.

"Get on her," Kate called.

"Hold on," I said impatiently.

"Are you scared?"

"Probably," I answered. "It's kinda hard to tell at the moment."

I put my arm on Lizzy's neck and leaned into her. She smelled kind of like corn chips. She didn't move so I lifted my right leg and gently jumped onto her lowered neck. I slid back and came to a stop just above her front legs. She lifted her head and I grabbed onto one of the round ridges growing from the back of her neck.

Lizzy straightened out her powerful front legs and stood up on all fours. She cocked her head and began to walk directly toward Kate. With just three great steps, Lizzy was standing directly in front of Kate. Kate's shoulders and arms were shaking.

Lizzy opened her mouth and snorted, and Kate wobbled like she was going to pass out. I wasn't actually happy about this, but Kate was usually so cool and unfrazzled that it was kind of interesting to see her shaking. Kate stood her ground and grimaced at Lizzy. I had always imagined that someday two girls might fight over me. I just hadn't thought that one of them would literally be able to bite the other one's head off and then fly away.

I glanced down at Kate as she gazed up at me.

"You think you're pretty cool, don't you?" she said mockingly.

"Just a little," I smiled and tossed my hair back.

Lizzy walked around the edge of the cavern three times with me on her back. I felt privileged just to be near her. I could see the huge hole she had dug in the middle of the cavern. It looked like an empty dirt swimming pool. None of the other dragons had ever nested like that.

At the end of the third trip around Lizzy stopped, lowered her head, and leaned to the right so that I slid off of her. She looked at me and almost smiled—at least that's how I perceived it. She then nudged me with her head, screeched, and with one fantastic leap leaped toward the cavern's ceiling. She twisted her body as she darted and rocketed feet first with her wings folded in. The blue talons on her back legs grabbed the stone roof and held fast.

Her body dangled like a white uvula.

Kate stepped up to me and put her arm around my waist.

"She's incredible," Kate said in awe. "But scary."

"You're just jealous," I replied.

"So what do we do with her?"

"Whaddya mean?" I asked.

"I thought you were supposed to destroy her."

"No way," I insisted. "That guy lied about other things, and I'm not going to just take his word for it."

"So what happens?" Kate asked passionately. "I mean, she can't stay in this cave forever."

"Why not?"

"Don't be stupid, Beck. What if she keeps getting bigger?"

"I don't know," I answered with frustration. "But I'm not going to harm her. Look at her."

We both stared at Lizzy as she slightly swayed.

"I guess you don't know how to kill her anyway," Kate said, defeated.

"Actually I do," I told her.

"How?"

"I'm not saying."

"What?"

"I'm not saying," I repeated myself. "It wouldn't be right."

"It's not like I'm actually going to use the information," Kate argued.

"Still," I lamely argued back.

"Listen, Beck," she said. "I think Lizzy's amazing. I haven't really thought about much else since I first saw her. And now I don't think I'll think of anything else. But remember what happened last time?"

"This is different," I insisted.

"How?"

"There were more dragons," I said waving my arms. "And none of them were the queen. I'm pretty sure there's some law somewhere that says you can't kill a queen."

"You're quite the debater," Kate said insultingly.

"Thanks," I sniffed.

"This is ridiculous. What are you going to do? Just live in here with her?"

"Maybe."

Kate shut her blue eyes and then opened them slowly. I could see the depth and a swirling energy in them. They didn't pop like Lizzy's, but they weren't bad. Kate turned and walked toward the sliding steel door.

My shoulders drooped, and I sighed. "Come on, Kate, don't go."

Kate stopped and turned her head. "Are you going to tell me?"

"It's not that easy," I argued. "I can't just . . ."

Kate kept walking.

"Kate."

She stepped through the door and out of sight. I stood there for almost half an hour waiting for her to grow up and come back.

Apparently she liked being a child.

Illustration from page 47 of The Grim Knot

CHAPTER 20

Action Right Now

I REMEMBER WHEN I WAS A child reading a book about a boy and a fish. The story went like this. A boy went into a pet shop and bought a fish. Before he left the pet shop the owner told the boy to not feed the fish too much. The wise boy, knowing that sometimes people said things that weren't true, promptly went home and fed the fish a whole box of food. Well, almost instantly the fish grew too big for the fish bowl so the boy moved him to the tub. Then the fish grew too big for the bathtub, so he moved him to a pool. I don't remember what happens after that. I think they had a huge neighborhood barbecue and everyone ate part of the fish. And although I can't clearly remember the end, that story reminds me of Lizzy.

The day after Kate immaturely stormed out on me, Lizzy was a good bit bigger. The next day she was bigger than that, and the following three days she kept right on growing. By the end of the week she was too big for me to climb onto, unless she let me scale her tail and shimmy up her back.

She was frightening, but I was so taken with her I didn't care.

Another problem was that she was going through food like a pig with a high metabolism. She could polish off a whole barrel of the dragon cereal in three bites. And after each bite I could practically see her size increase.

Still, she was perfect.

I hated being away from her. I had a hard time sleeping. It bothered me to have to take time to eat, and I felt great pain every time I had to lock that steel door behind me and hike back home.

Luckily the rain had finally stopped, and it was forecasted that we might actually have sun mixed with clouds for the next two weeks. Things were beginning to dry out, and it was much easier to get up to the cave.

I was still waiting for Kate to grow up. I figured now that it had stopped raining she would come over and apologize for walking out—she didn't. I even swallowed my pride and called her once, acting like I was one of her teachers. But her mom said she couldn't come to the phone because she was meditating. Likely story—what kind of person younger than Buddha meditates?

The best news was that my dad came home. I went up to visit him a couple of times, but his thoughts were so preoccupied that he barely noticed me. I didn't mention a thing about Lizzy because I was afraid he would go all legal-guardian on me. And since he had a really difficult time carrying on a conversation, or asking me about my life, it never came up. I did ask him where he had been. His answer was, "Putting something to rest." It sounded like gangster-talk so I let it go.

Millie was happy my father was back in the manor—which made me happy because she spent less time fussing over me—which left me more time to spend with Lizzy.

I was walking through the courtyard, making my way to the train tracks, when I plowed into Wane as she came around the corner of the house. We collided and bounced apart from each other.

"Sorry," I said.

"Don't worry about it," she replied, rubbing her nose that I had knocked with my chin. "Where are you racing to?"

"I'm thinking of catching grasshoppers." It was all I could come up with on the spot, so I ran with it.

"Really?" Wane asked in surprise.

I decided to dig my hole deeper. "Yep, maybe I'll catch them and then name them and then track them."

"You can track grasshoppers?"

"It's not easy," I said, bothered by how lame an excuse I had come up with. "What's your hurry?" I asked, throwing it back to her.

"I was coming to find you," she answered.

"Why?"

"Because I just talked to the sheriff."

That was not a line any kid ever wanted to hear. My mind started racing with all the things I could have done wrong to make the sheriff call Wane.

"I didn't do . . ."

"Listen, Beck," Wane interrupted. "It wasn't about you. Sheriff Pax told me that the road's almost fixed."

"Okay," I said relieved.

"They say it should be done by tonight."

"Right."

"You'll be going back to school," Wane clarified. "Is there anything you'll need?"

"School?" I asked, as if she had just introduced a completely new word to my vocabulary.

"School," she reiterated.

My stomach sank down into my right leg, bobbed back up

into my throat, and then settled in my gut like a heavy meal. I had actually missed school a week ago, but now I could think of nothing more horrible than having to spend the day at Callowbrow while Lizzy was up in the cave being her amazing self.

"I can't go to school," I panicked.

"Why?" Wane asked.

"Kids there pick on me," I whined urgently.

She wasn't buying it. "Beck, you're bigger than almost any of the boys there, and quicker."

"But I'm not as crafty," I argued.

"I don't know anybody craftier," she said, folding her arms.

"The sheriff shouldn't be calling you," I tried, clinging to the thinnest of hopes. "He's got more important things to do than to bother you."

"The phone call's already happened, Beck. So as concerned as you are about Sheriff Pax and his schedule, it doesn't matter now."

"I have a school library fine," I said, grasping at straws.

"Your school doesn't have a library," Wane informed me.

"They don't?"

Wane shook her head. "Actually, they do, but it's obvious you've never visited it. You're going to school tomorrow," she insisted. "Sheriff Pax said the bus should be right on time."

I didn't know what to do. Suddenly it felt as if all my time had been sucked away from me. I had plans—plans to hang out with Lizzy. Most of the world didn't even believe in dragons, and I had one hidden away who needed all my attention.

"I wanna be homeschooled," I blurted out.

"Come on, Beck."

"Honest," I said. "I feel I can get a much better education that way. I'll buy some flashcards and you can teach me how to play chess. Plus, we can all sleep in."

"Nice try," Wane smiled. "You're going to Callowbrow tomorrow." Wane walked off laughing.

I ran to the train tracks, through the woods, up the stairs, and into the cave. I turned on the lights, rolled open the steel door, closed it behind me, and then collapsed on the dirt. I could hear Lizzy drop from the ceiling, and I felt the ground tremor as she strode over.

"Sorry, Liz," I said breathing hard. "Let me catch my breath."

Lizzy stepped right up to me and tilted her head down to make eye contact. She snorted and dragon drool splattered all over my face.

"Nice," I said, trying to be kind. I looked up. Her huge blue eyes were like cobalt tar pits that seized my gaze. Her head was the size of a couch and the scales around her eyes reflected light down on me like a disco ball.

I wiped off my face with the back of my arm.

Lizzy yawned and I got a perfect glimpse of her frighteningly large teeth and purple tongue. I could also see down her throat and I realized that if she decided to, she could bite me in half with just one chomp.

I rolled over and got on my hands and knees. I then stood and dusted myself off. Lizzy butted her head against the steel door.

"What?" I asked her. "You wanna get out?"

Lizzy scratched at the ground and screeched.

"Honestly," I said holding my ears. "You're going to make me go deaf."

She head butted the door again.

"You can't go out," I insisted. "It's not safe."

I think even she, with her low dragon intellect, knew how ridiculous it sounded for me to be saying something like that to her—she was too large to worry about safety.

I was going to go on about how she shouldn't leave, when a small warm thought began to spread over me. It started at my toes, and in a few moments my entire body was tingling. The Pillage in me was awakening.

"You know what, why not?" I asked myself.

Lizzy was so powerful and so awe inspiring. I couldn't imagine a single thing in the world being able to really bother her.

And I couldn't imagine any of those same things bothering me while I was with her. I had stopped thinking soundly.

I fetched a large rope that was coiled up on top of a crate. I tossed it over Lizzy's neck and back up. I then wove it behind her two front legs and beneath the spot her wings came out. I tied the only knot I knew—a square knot—and pulled her to the metal door.

"Come on," I said sliding the huge door open.

She ducked her head and moved forward. The opening was barely big enough for her to fit through. She stood up tall next to the train. I was amazed to see she was almost half the size of the big metal machine and her head reached way above the large metal scaffolding that the train was sitting under.

"Wow, there's no way you're going to fit through the opening to the outside."

I bolted to the moss and began pulling at the opening with my hands. Small bits of thick wet goo broke off. Lizzy lumbered over and shoved her head through the opening. As she lifted her neck up she created a dragon-sized hole in the tall green wall. She pulled her head back in and shook wet slime everywhere.

After wiping a piece of the sticky stuff off my face, I climbed up her tail and onto her back. I wrapped my hands and wrists around the rope hold and held on tightly.

"Ready?" I asked encouragingly.

Lizzy snorted and pawed at the dirt like a bull.

I yelled the only thing I could think of, "Yah!"

It worked. Lizzy stomped through the opening, tearing it even wider. She stood on the stone ledge in front of the cave and opened her wings. It was so impressive that I felt like clapping, but I kept my grip, knowing what was coming next.

Lizzy sprang out from behind the crooked trees and into the semi-blue sky. I could feel wind racing up my nose, and my heart was beating in such a way that I thought it was going to pop out of my chest and smack me in the face.

I missed this.

There had been few things in my life as exciting as the moments I had been able to ride on a flying dragon. It just doesn't get much better. Ever since the first dragons had begun their pillage and I had been able to hitch a ride back and forth into town on one, I had hoped that I would get the chance to ride one again someday. Now as Lizzy rocketed higher and higher, I felt as if I would pass out from happiness.

Lizzy leveled out, just short of the stratosphere. My lungs lurched and huffed for more oxygen as my body froze. I would have worried, but Lizzy hunched and began angling downward. We shot to the earth, my heels digging into her scales above her wings and my eyes wide open. We buzzed the manor and then whizzed over the rockslide and the open prairie on the opposite side. .

Lizzy flapped her wings and we ascended above the west mountains. She cleared the jagged peaks and dipped down into a beautiful green valley I didn't know existed. We wove through clouds and skimmed the earth like water bugs on a glass lake. I wanted my father to be here with me. I wanted Kate to look up and see what she was missing. I wanted Wyatt to be jealous, and I wanted the flight to never end.

It was perfect.

I could see a quaint chapel with a tin roof sitting on the edge of a dark blue pond down below. The scene was so serene and intoxicating I felt dizzy. I breathed in and the smell of wintergreen filled my nostrils. I then closed my eyes and listened to Lizzy's massive wings flap up and down. Much like the sound of the ocean, it was a noise I don't think I could ever get sick of.

Lizzy screamed, and every bird in the sky went stock-still and fell toward the ground. I held my face up to the sun and the racing wind and contemplated how lucky I was.

When I opened my eyes we were considerably closer to the small white chapel. The tin roof glistened in the patchy sunlight, blinding me for a moment. Lizzy continued to fly straight toward it at a remarkable speed.

"Wait a second," I yelled. "You're not going to . . ."

I had to interrupt what I was asking so that I could execute a proper scream. Lizzy slammed into the roof, her talons ripping off the top of the chapel's bell tower. The sound of splitting wood and snapping metal bounced from cloud to cloud and filled the entire sky. I could see the church bell slide down the pitched tin roof and clank against the ground.

Lizzy flapped her powerful wings and clawed her way up into the sky. She turned her head and circled around again.

"You can't . . ."

My screaming wouldn't let me get a word in edgewise.

Lizzy swooped toward the chapel as I hung on for my life. Her talons grasped the peak of the tin roof and, with a tremendous howl and a deep grunt, she ripped off half the covering. She carried the tin roofing in her talons and screamed. I looked down and could see directly into the chapel. With half the roof gone, I could see an organ with brass pipes. There was a little gray-haired lady sitting at the organ, staring up at where the ceiling once was.

Lizzy turned and spotted the shiny organ pipes. She instantly dropped the tin roofing and shot straight down. The old woman clutched her chest and screamed like they used to do in old-fashioned movies. She fell backward off the organ bench as we dropped in.

Lizzy spun and grabbed the pipes with her back talons. She

then added something new to the mix by breathing fire and igniting a third of the chapel.

"No!" I screamed as heat pummeled me.

But Lizzy ignored me, turning her head as she swept fire everywhere. I held tightly to the ropes, wishing I were back in the cave.

Lizzy leaped out of the burning building with half the organ pipes clenched tightly in her talons. I could see the old woman frantically running from the church, as flames engulfed the entire structure.

I suddenly felt like throwing up.

Lizzy screeched and then straightened out her head and flew in the direction of the manor. I wanted to think, or say something to make myself feel better, but both my brain and my mouth were speechless.

We soared over the mountains and into the Hagen Valley as I clung to the ropes, wishing the ride would end. Lizzy raced across the landscape, the scenery splashing by me. We were going so fast my cheeks were flapping and my skin was cold. Lizzy lifted up and headed straight for the cave. She screeched as she flew over the manor. I could see the copper dome and then the train tracks down between the trees.

Lizzy threaded herself in through the moss door and dropped the pipes on the dirt in front of the stationary train.

They clanged and scattered over the train tracks. I slipped off Lizzy and fell face first into the soil.

"What were you thinking?" I yelled as I got up. "You tore that church apart."

Lizzy blinked her eyes and rocked back and forth. She looked both proud and embarrassed.

"You need to get back into your cave," I insisted. "Now."

She lowered her head and scooped up the organ pipes with her mouth. My stomach was twisting and lurching. I pulled on her ropes and tried to fit her through the steel door but the pipes were too long.

"Can't you just drop them?"

She cocked her head.

I pulled the rope back, helping her thread the pipes through the door sideways. As soon as she was all the way in I walked out and rolled the door shut behind her. I threw the heavy metal latch into place, locking her up.

"This is not good."

I leaned my back against the door and moaned. I could hear Lizzy tossing the organ pipes around and screeching triumphantly.

"Let's just hope nobody noticed."

It was extremely wishful thinking on my part.

Illustration from page 50 of The Grim Knot

CHAPTER 21

Put Out the Fire

HEN I GOT BACK TO THE manor it was almost dark and I was so worried and out of sorts I almost didn't recognize myself. I looked in the mirror hanging on the wall near the kitchen and was surprised to see it was still me.

I crept past the open kitchen door hoping to go unrecognized by Millie as well.

"Get in here, Beck," she called.

I leaned my head back and looked in. "Yes?"

"Come," she insisted.

"I was going to go to bed," I told her. "I want to get a good sleep for tomorrow since the road is fixed."

"Get in here."

I walked into the kitchen with my head down. Millie was

really the closest thing I had to family, aside from my dad. She was like a grandma-mother-aunt hybrid, and I could tell by the tone of her voice that I was in trouble.

"Your father's angry," she said. "I'm not sure why, but he's in a mood."

"Really?" I asked. "You're not sure why?"

"He rang for you to come up some time ago, and he's been ringing every ten minutes since then."

"He could just come down himself," I suggested.

"I agree," Millie complained. "Wane and I have been running up and down those stairs like mad women just to tell him you're not back yet."

"Sorry," I apologized.

"I should make you rub my knees," Millie said.

"That doesn't seem totally fair," I complained.

Millie grumbled and then pointed for me to go.

"So I'm supposed to go see him?"

"Now," she insisted.

I was even more worried and more out of sorts by the time I reached my father's door. It felt like my stomach had the flu and it was throwing up into my lungs.

I knocked and then pushed open the door. My father was sitting in his chair staring at the floor. I closed the door behind me.

"You wanted to see me?" I asked quietly.

"Come in," he said.

I looked around, wondering how much more "in" I could come.

"I'm sick," he said without looking up.

"Me too," I replied sincerely. "I guess I'm nervous about going back to school."

"Beck," he scolded. "I saw the dragon in the sky."

"I like to spot neat-shaped clouds too," I tried.

My father stomped his right foot. "It wasn't the clouds. I saw a dragon. A white queen."

I had no choice but to tell him. "She's locked up now," I said defensively. "I'm sorry, I didn't think . . ."

"It's no good," he interrupted. "She'll think of nothing but pillaging now."

"That's not true," I said, defending her. "Lizzy's different."

"Lizzy?"

"She had to have a name," I told him.

"No she didn't," he barked.

He lifted his head and stood. He then did one of the things that bothered me most, he paced along the windows looking out and talking as if he were having the conversation with the clouds and not me. "You hatched a dragon."

"Oops," I said humbly.

"Oops?" he said, repeating what I had just said. "Oops?"

"Sorry," I tried.

"It was done," he mourned. "It was over."

"I didn't mean to," I apologized. "Honest."

"You didn't mean to what?" he asked sternly, towering over me, the ends of his long nightshirt billowing lightly. "You didn't mean to find the stone among the millions of stones?"

"Well . . ."

"You didn't mean to then plant the stone?" he continued, not even giving me a second to answer.

"I . . ."

"It was by mistake that you harvested it?" he said scornfully. "And then, quite by accident, you raised it and let it loose?"

"Well, when you put it that way, it does sort of make me look bad."

My dad massaged his forehead as if there were a tattoo there he was hoping to rub off.

"Beck," he sighed.

"Dad," I said manipulatively.

"This is on your head," he whispered. "What the queen pillages will be the work of her talons and your hands."

I looked at my hands, marveling at all the trouble they were capable of getting me into.

"The old man told me I had to," I said. "I thought it was what I needed to do."

"But what else did he say?"

"He said to destroy her while she was small."

"That was not a small dragon I saw flying in the air." My father paced back and forth, his entire body shaking.

"It's fine," I told him. "She's locked up and can't harm anyone. I'll make sure of it."

My father fell back into his chair. He closed his eyes, looking as if the entire world had just punched him in the gut.

"I'm a terrible father," he whispered.

"It's not like I'm a perfect son," I said trying to make him feel better.

"Go," he waved.

"Dad," I whined.

"Just go."

I went to my room and lay on my bed on my stomach with my face pushed into the pillow and my arms by my side. I wanted the guilt in *my* gut to go away. I had let down Kate, myself, and my father. Plus, somewhere there was a little gray-haired organist most likely having a heart attack by now.

I screamed into my pillow as someone knocked on my door.

"Go away," I yelled nicely.

"Beck, it's Wane," she called.

I rolled over. "I'm sleeping."

"Beck," Wane hollered sternly. "Sheriff Pax is downstairs, and he needs to talk to you."

I stood up and opened the door. Wane was standing there wearing an expression that didn't exactly flatter her normally pretty face.

"The sheriff?" I asked nervously.

Wane nodded.

"Is it about the school bus coming tomorrow?" I asked hopefully.

"I don't think so."

I spent the rest of the night talking to Sheriff Pax. Apparently that little gray-haired lady who had been practicing the organ—the same one I had selflessly worried over—had gone straight to the police and described the incident. It took me a long time to convince Sheriff Pax that even if she was telling the truth, I had nothing to do with it.

"Something's not right," he said. "That woman was a church organist, why would she lie?"

"I know a grandmother who stole a car," I argued, stretching the truth a bit more. I didn't actually know said grandmother, but I had read about it in a book.

Sheriff Pax wrote something down on his police notebook.

"Hundreds of people here have blamed things on dragons,"

I went on. "Ever since that last incident, tons of crazy people have made things up."

"Well, something tore off the roof of that church," Sheriff Pax said with authority. "Part of it was laying hundreds of feet away."

"Maybe it exploded, and the roof blew off," I told him, making a few things up myself. I knew it was wrong, but there was no way I was giving Lizzy up.

"Listen, Beck," he said, staring at me. "This is an active investigation. I don't want you telling anybody about any of this until we have more information."

I crossed my heart.

"If I find out you've lied to me, there will be severe consequences," he warned. "And I'm not sure even the Pillage name will save you. Now, you're positive there's not something you want to tell me?"

"All right," I sighed in defeat. "When I was eight, I stole my neighbor's hose and used it as a swinging vine."

The sheriff closed his pad and growled at me. "That sharp tongue is going to get you in trouble someday."

"Believe me," I lamented. "It already has."

I could have been wrong, but I think I saw a small smile on his face.

He handed me a business card and promised me he would

be back soon to check on me and my story. His promise wasn't all that comforting.

I called Kate right before I went to sleep. Nobody answered. It might have been because they somehow knew it was me calling or maybe it was because it was after eleven o'clock. Either way, my head now hurt right along with my body and soul.

"This stinks."

Despite the fact that I had flown on the back of a dragon earlier in the day, I don't think I had ever felt lower.

Illustration from page 54 of The Grim Knot

CHAPTER 22

Waiting for the Hammer to Fall

I TRIED MY BEST TO GET OUT OF going to school. I woke up and instantly started coughing. When Wane came by to make sure I was up, I coughed extra hard. I thought she looked sympathetic until she told me that if I coughed once more she was going to reach down my throat and try to repair my lungs personally.

"I think I'm feeling better," I said.

"I thought so," she replied.

While eating a breakfast of cream-covered fruit and massive blueberry muffins dripping with butter, I kept moaning and grumbling so Millie would think I was ill and make me stay home. Unfortunately, she just mistook my noises as a compliment about her cooking.

As I shuffled down the driveway, I felt defeated and

uncomfortable. I looked up toward the mountains. Thanks to all the trees growing out sideways, I couldn't see the cave or any sign of the moss opening. I considered just ditching school and going to hang out with Lizzy, but I knew that would only make Sheriff Pax and my family more suspicious.

I stood by the gate waiting for the bus and wishing I made better decisions in my life. I looked up at the three gargoyles on the gate shack—even they looked mad at me. It was early in the day, but already I had the feeling that something else bad was about to happen. I felt like I was watching a movie where I knew that any moment something awful was going to take place. Of course, the big difference was that I couldn't pause my life or rewind to a point where I could fix the mess I had made.

When the school bus finally arrived, I got on reluctantly. Kate was sitting in a seat next to a boy I knew she hated. I waved at her, but she looked away. Things were obviously worse than I had thought. I sat down in the seat directly behind her.

"Hey, Kate."

She didn't answer.

"Something happened with that big girl we know," I said using code again.

Kate got up from where she was sitting and moved four rows closer to the front of the bus. The boy she had been sitting by turned around and looked at me.

"She said you were a jerk," he told me.

"Thanks."

My stomach grew even more unsettled.

When we got to Callowbrow, Kate rushed off the bus, and I never caught up to her. To make matters worse she wasn't at lunch, and I had to sit by Wyatt and a boy who didn't wear deodorant.

"So what'd you do to tick Kate off?" Wyatt asked.

I took a tiny bite of my sandwich, spit it out because nothing tasted good at the moment, and said, "I'm not sure."

"Girls," Wyatt scoffed. "*You* can't live with 'em and you can't live without them, because *they* all wanna be with me."

"Give it up, Wyatt," I said, setting my sandwich down.

"You're just jealous," he replied starting in on his own lunch.

Kate came into the cafeteria ten minutes later and walked right past us. I watched her buy an apple from the cafeteria lady and then leave through the far doors.

"I'm in trouble," I moaned.

"Don't worry about it," Wyatt said. "Not everyone can be as smooth with the ladies as I am." He patted me on the back, and I had to resist the urge to hit him.

I used the remainder of my lunch period to write a note to Kate. It was over a page long and said a number of things that

I probably couldn't express well verbally. I was desperate. I gave the note to Wyatt so he could deliver it to her next period when he had science with Kate. I made him swear not to open it and read it.

"Too juicy for me to read," he said, raising his eyebrows.

"No, but the words are probably too big for you to understand."

The rest of the day was long and filled with teachers dishing out tons of makeup homework that the washed-out road had caused. I should have paid better attention, but all I could think about was Kate and Lizzy. It was weird to have girl problems that concerned two different species. By the time my last class ended I was determined to find Kate and do whatever it took to convince her that I was honestly sorry. Hopefully she had read my note and her feelings toward me were already softening.

When Kate wasn't at her locker, I decided to wait for her at the bus. While walking there I heard someone calling my name. I wanted it to be Kate, but the voice was too low.

"Beck!"

I tried not to appear overeager as I looked about, just in case whoever was yelling was actually calling someone else.

"Beck!"

I spotted the yeller across the street and beneath an enormous willow tree. It was Van and he was still wearing a blue hoodie. We made eye contact but I quickly looked down, pretending not to notice.

"Beck!" I could hear him running across the street. His shadow mixed with mine and I finally looked up.

"What?" I said, bothered.

"I need to talk to you," Van smiled. "For just a moment. I think it will be worth your time."

I looked at the school bus and still saw no sign of Kate.

"I should yell 'stranger,'" I told him. "Then maybe they'd take you away and lock you up."

Van laughed. "I actually left for a couple of days, but then I got the oddest call."

"I can only imagine what kind of people call you."

"Funny, Beck," he laughed. "Always funny. You know what's not funny?"

"Reporters," I answered.

"No," he said, ignoring my sarcasm. "What's not funny is when someone or something burns down a church."

I could see Van watching me for a reaction, but I didn't give him one. I just stared at him until he cleared his throat.

"Oh," I said as if confused. "That was your point? You just came here to tell me that burning churches isn't funny? You're quite the journalist. What's tomorrow's headline going to be, 'Making fun of sick people isn't nice?'"

"It was a dragon," he whispered fiercely. "A dragon burnt down that church, Beck."

"Aren't you a little old to believe in dragons?" I asked, while still keeping my eyes open for any sign of Kate.

"I have friends on the police force," he informed me in a low voice. I think he was trying to sound threatening. "I know things. You need to talk to me, Beck."

"Listen, Van," I said as nicely as I could. "I know you think I'm hiding some great secret from you, but I don't know what you're talking about."

Van grabbed the front of my shirt and almost instantly realized this was not the right spot to do something like that. He let go and tried to smile as students continued to stream past us. I had been bothered by Van, but up until that moment when I witnessed the rage in his eyes, I had never been scared of him.

I stepped back. "You should go."

"Beck, I want to help," he huffed. "This could change everything for both me and you. Is it money you want?"

I laughed at him.

"I can help you, Beck," he hissed.

"I don't want your help," I said loudly. My raised voice caused a number of students to look over at us. "Leave me and my family alone."

"Keep your voice down," he demanded in a whisper. "You're making a huge mistake—one that might hurt you in the end."

I didn't know what to do. My sick stomach was not absorbing the threat very well. I wished so badly that I could throw up on him, but I just didn't have it in me.

"You need my help," he insisted.

"Go to . . ." The bus horn beeped right on time.

I turned around and stormed off, trying to look cool. I was mad, and I knew that everyone was staring at me. I got onto the bus, walked down the aisle, and sat in one of the back seats. I felt angry, cool, and confused. I also felt stupid because the second the vehicle started moving, I realized that I had accidentally gotten on the wrong bus. I rode it to the first stop and then got off and called Thomas.

I had to beg Thomas for a full five minutes before he agreed to come into town and pick me up. I then just stood in front of the pay phone, looking like a traveler who had no money and nowhere to go.

My heart hurt.

I guess the one good thing about my mistake was that because of the waiting I now had time to mentally list and think about all the things that were going wrong. Of course it was the kind of good thing that only a grown-up would appreciate.

Illustration from page 60 of The Grim Knot

CHAPTER 23

Stone Cold Wacko

B Y THE TIME I FINALLY GOT home it was dinnertime. I ate a bunch of delicious food and then excused myself to go and do all of my makeup homework. Which, loosely translated, meant I was going to see Lizzy.

I took the secret passage from behind the mirror and exited the manor from the hidden door near the courtyard. I ran through the dusk and into the forest. By the time I got to the Lizzie-size hole in the moss wall it was almost completely dark outside.

I turned the lights on and practically skipped to the large steel door. I'd apologize for the skipping, but it had been a full day since I had seen Lizzy and I was going through withdrawals.

I undid the heavy metal latch and rolled the steel door open just enough for me to slip through. I didn't want there to be any chance of Lizzy getting out. I slipped in and rolled the door shut. When I turned around I couldn't see any sign of her. The organ pipes she had stolen were stacked almost neatly in a pile near the cocoon.

"Lizzy!"

Once again the dirt in the center of the cavern began to rise. Unlike before, however, something was different. I could see Lizzy's white scales, but now patches of her were gray and black. She rose out of the dirt screeching wildly. Soil tumbled off of her like dirty lava as she spread her wings and flapped them. Dirt flew everywhere—a small fist of soil smacked me in the left ear. Despite the hit, I kept my eyes trained on her. She looked my direction and screeched, fire spreading out in front of her mouth like a giant flaming flower. She snapped her jaws shut and stood there staring at me as smoke drifted up from her nostrils.

"Wow," I whispered.

I walked up to her with my right hand out in front of me and gently took hold of the rope around her neck.

"Come on," I said attempting to pull her in the direction of the water. She pulled back, jerking the rope. "Seriously, Lizzy, come on."

She let me walk her to the water but she had an attitude

about it. She took a few drinks and then looked at me like she was angry.

"What?" I argued. "I'm trying to help. It just seems that if I was a dragon and I had just spit up fire that my throat would be a little parched."

She turned around and snorted. Then with an air of great purpose, she began stepping across the cavern and toward the steel door. I held onto the rope as I walked alongside her.

"Listen," I reasoned. "Just so we're clear, we can't go flying out there anymore. But there's plenty of space in here for you to mess around."

She just kept on walking.

"You got me busted," I told her. "There were cops at my house."

Lizzy growled.

"What?" I said defensively. "I didn't give you up. It was that old lady with the gray hair."

We reached the door, and Lizzy stopped. She lowered her head and gazed at the large metal latch.

"Stare all you want," I told her. "I'm not opening it. You can't . . ."

There was a knock on the door. Lizzy looked as surprised as me. We both stepped back. The knock was soft.

"Should I open it?" I asked.

Dragons are so useless when it comes to conversation.

"Who is it?" I yelled.

There was some muffled yelling but I couldn't tell who it was or what they were saying. I slid the bolt back and then lifted it up. The door began to roll open.

"Kate?"

She slipped in, and I quickly closed the door again. Lizzy wasn't happy about me shutting the door. She started stomping her feet and thrashing her tail about.

"What's up with her?" Kate asked.

"She wants to get out," I explained. "But who cares about that. You came."

Kate smiled at me with both her eyes and her lips. "Your note was nice. I didn't want it to, but it made me laugh."

"That was a serious note," I complained.

"I know."

Lizzy screeched and dug at the dirt with her horns.

"I really am sorry," I said. "You more than anyone should know how much I want to be a better person."

"I know, and I'm still mad at you," Kate explained. "But, to be honest, I've been dying to see Lizzy."

Lizzy began to butt up against the steel door with her horns. The solid structure didn't even shake under the pressure of her weight. She started slamming up against it harder. Both Kate and I stepped back.

"Is she okay?" Kate asked.

Lizzy screamed and began clawing at the bolt with her talons. At first it was kind of interesting, but after a couple of seconds it grew frightening. She looked over at me and screeched.

Kate and I plugged our ears and cowered in perfect synchronicity. Lizzy blew flames at the door, but all her efforts weren't making a bit of difference.

Lizzy turned her head and looked directly at me.

"She really wants you to open the door," Kate said.

"She'll fly out and destroy something," I told her. "She burnt down a church yesterday."

Lizzy began butting at the door again.

"Maybe *we* should go out then," Kate suggested. "She seems a little mental."

I was going to point out to Kate that her idea, while valid, was easier said than done. Lizzy was currently blocking our only exit.

"We could go through the back tunnel," Kate suggested.

"What about the moths?" I questioned in worry. "Listen, Lizzy will be okay. We just need to distract her from the door."

Lizzy was looking at me again. I took the opportunity to try and talk kindly to her. "All right, Lizzy. Let's just move you back to your nest."

I slowly stepped up toward her and reached out to grab the rope. She snapped her huge jaw at me and I jumped back quickly.

"What the . . ."

Lizzy opened her mouth and screamed.

"Come on, Beck," Kate said urgently, tugging on the back of my shirt.

Lizzy stood up on her hind feet and threw the front of her body down, causing the ground to shake. Kate was no longer tugging. She was running. I decided to follow her example and set off across the cavern in a different direction. Lizzy screamed even louder, and I could hear the flap of her massive wings behind me.

"Beck!" Kate screamed.

I dived behind a row of crates and crawled frantically across the dirt. Lizzy slammed into the crates, sending them flying everywhere. One flew over my head and smashed into the stone wall next to me. Lizzy screamed and stood on her hind legs again. I could see that Kate had made it to the metal door. She was behind Lizzy and sliding the bolt open. She looked in my direction and waved me over. I tried to nod in such a way that she would know to just get out and I'd come later.

I guess she understood me because she started to roll the

door open. As she did so, the latch swung down making a clanking noise. Lizzy spun around and saw Kate. She screamed so loud, bits of rock began to fall from the ceiling. Kate slipped out and heaved the door shut just as Lizzy slammed into it. She clawed and scratched angrier than she had ever been.

I used the distraction to get up and scramble for my life. I knew I only had a couple of seconds so I jumped into one of the empty dragon cereal barrels and slid the top over me. There was a small open knothole on the side, and I was able to wedge my head down just enough to see out of it. I didn't have a clear view of the whole cavern, but I could see Lizzy and some of the other barrels lined up near me.

Lizzy turned and snorted in my direction. Her head swung side to side as she gazed around the cavern. She looked like a dragon pendulum. I tried to slow my breathing. Inside the barrel my breaths echoed louder and louder. I knew if she found me that it would be bad, and I was hoping that the strong smell of dragon cereal everywhere would hide my scent.

Lizzy stormed over, tearing at the crates in her way. She stopped in front of the row of barrels and leaned her head down to sniff one that was three barrels away from me. I held my breath, willing her to go away. She nudged the top of the barrel and then stopped. I was thinking my plan just might work when suddenly she turned and slammed her tail down against the barrel. The wooden vessel shattered into a million pieces sending dragon cereal and wood slivers flying everywhere. If my bladder were any weaker, I would have been sitting in a wet drum.

Lizzy moved to the next barrel. She sniffed at it and then pulled back her head and screamed. I held my breath as Lizzy let loose with a tremendous plume of fire. The vat was instantly consumed in flame.

I was going to die.

Lizzy stepped up to the barrel right next to me and sniffed. I held perfectly still, feeling like that one lady in the movie where they were hiding from Nazis and there was a lot of singing.

Lizzy sniffed the vat again and then rose up on her back feet. She picked up the barrel, and threw it against the stone wall. I couldn't see where it hit, but I could hear the explosion of wood and see the shrapnel raining down.

Lizzy lowered her body and sidestepped in front of my vat. It took everything I had to keep my body from shaking. I kept wishing Kate would do something to distract her. Or maybe Kate could open up the huge metal door, and Lizzy could fly out and ruin the entire town of Kingsplot instead of me.

Lizzy sniffed at the top of my barrel. I could see her scaly underside through the hole I was looking out of. I couldn't control my shaking and my teeth began to chatter.

She sniffed once more, and I stopped breathing altogether.

Illustration from page 63 of The Grim Knot

CHAPTER 24

Keep Yourself Alive

I HAD ONE OF THREE WAYS TO DIE. One: be obliterated by Lizzy's tail. Two: be burned. Three: be thrown against the wall and busted up. Any way I looked at it, I was in trouble. My heart was beating so fast I thought it was going to jump out of my chest and start bouncing around the inside of the barrel.

I closed my eyes and tried to enjoy watching my life flash before my eyes. Lizzy screamed, and I knew I was done for. I breathed in deep and whimpered.

Lizzy screamed again, and I could hear her massive wings flap. I opened my eyes and looked out through the hole. There were shadows and dark, blurring images everywhere. Lizzy was hopping up and down and blowing fire. I couldn't believe it.

"Moths," I whispered excitedly.

The cavern was filling up with them and they were

distracting Lizzy. I was trying to figure out how the back door had gotten open, when the lid of my barrel popped off. I was a little surprised to see who was there.

"Van?" I questioned in disbelief.

"Hurry," he whispered as moths covered his face. "We don't have much time."

Van pulled me out of the barrel as we were swarmed by the dirty, winged insects. Lizzy was flying around the other side of the cavern screaming and blowing. Fireballs flashed through the air as pockets of moths lit up and then fell to the ground smoking.

"Come on, Beck!" Van said as he pulled me along the side of the cavern toward the door. "Hurry!"

The moths were bad, but they were not quite as thick as the last time. I could see enough to view the large metal door and note that Kate was opening it about a foot wide. Unfortunately, I could also see that Lizzy was on to us.

"Run faster!" Van screamed.

Lizzy stomped through the moths and across the cavern racing toward us. The insects were everywhere, filling my eyes and mouth every time I opened either of them. Lizzy spread her wings and shot through the air just above the crates.

Van screamed something, but I couldn't understand him. He reached the door first and squeezed through the opening. I turned back for one last look, and there was Lizzy five feet away, lunging toward me. Van tugged my left arm and yanked me all the way through the door just as Kate closed it. There was a tremendous crash as Lizzy slammed into the other side of the metal door.

I fell to the ground choking and huffing. Van was right next to me rolling in the dirt and acting as if he were on fire. With the door closed, the bugs were next to nothing, although a few huddled around the lights on the wall or were flying out through the opening in the moss.

Kate helped me up. I reached out and gave Van a hand.

"Thanks," I said sheepishly.

"No problem," he replied.

I could hear Lizzy pitching a fit in the back cavern. She was screaming and beating against the door like a psycho dragon. We all took a few steps away from the door just to be safe.

"Who opened the back tunnel door anyway?" I asked.

"He did," Kate said, pointing toward Van. "It was my idea, but he crept in and opened the door. Luckily she was screaming so madly she didn't hear. I told Van which barrel you were in."

"Thanks," I said again. "I can't believe you did that."

"I told you," he smiled. "I'm here to help you."

I smiled back, sad that I had been such a jerk to him. "How did you even find us?"

Lizzy began to emit some sort of howlish cry.

"I was coming up your driveway hoping to speak with you when I saw a tiny string of light flicker on the side of this mountain. I started walking toward it and found the train tracks. I followed them and when I walked in, Kate was just coming out of that door."

"I keep telling Beck not to have the lights on at night," Kate said. "But, he's lucky he did, because there was no way I was going in there to save him."

"Thanks, Kate."

She kissed me on the cheek, making me feel better.

Lizzy was repeatedly pounding into the steel door. I grabbed the metal pin from off the dirt floor and slid it into the latch just to make sure she couldn't unlock it somehow.

"So what do we do now?" Kate asked.

"I don't want to, but we have to destroy her," I replied. "She'll tear apart everything. She was going to kill me."

"Sorry," Van said sympathetically. "I know this can't be easy for you."

I had totally misjudged Van.

"So how are we going to do it?" Kate asked as Lizzy screamed in the background and leftover moths drifted around us.

"Let's go in the train," Van suggested as he waved some

moths away. "I don't want even one of those bugs touching me again."

All three of us stepped into the train and took a seat where the passengers would have once sat.

"This is horrible," I lamented.

"I know," Kate agreed. "But we can't let her harm anyone. The other dragons didn't seem quite so possessed."

I put my head in my hands and moaned. "She just wants to pillage. My head's killing me."

"Hold on," Van said. "I think I have some aspirin in my backpack."

Van got up and walked off the train, closing the door behind him.

"I can't believe how wrong I was about him," I whispered to Kate. "Usually I'm such a good judge of character."

"Right," Kate smiled. "You just need to learn to . . ."

Kate stopped to look at something.

"Learn to what?" I asked as if the solution to all my troubles was in her answer. I turned to see where she was looking.

Her eyes were fixed on the door where Van had just exited. It was shut and through the small square windows we could both see him jamming a metal rod down through the door handle, locking us in.

Van looked in through the small window and smiled. "Kids are so foolish."

I jumped up before Kate.

"What are you doing?" I asked. "I thought you were getting your backpack."

"No," he answered. "What I'm doing is becoming the most famous person on earth."

"You can't do this," Kate reasoned.

"Already have," Van laughed.

I ran to the door and started to violently shake the handle and pound the door.

"Save your energy," Van insisted. "You'll get pretty weak in a few days without food or water."

I had totally misjudged Van . . . again!

"Come on, Van," I argued. "Let us out. My father . . . Thomas . . . well somebody will come looking for us."

"Maybe," he said. "I guess that depends upon how they feel after they read the note I forged, the one where you two talk about running off because you aren't allowed to be together."

Kate joined in on the banging. "Lizzy will kill you."

"I don't think so," he said, his smile oozing grease. "I'll get a tranquilizer gun. Shoot her full of enough medication to knock her out. Then, with the help of some of my more discreet friends, we'll move her out of here in the dark of night. I've already decided on the story about how I fought and captured her. Imagine, the world's first dragon in captivity."

"Let us out! A tranquilizer won't work on her," I yelled, not knowing for sure if it actually would. "Open this door!"

"How about you shut your trap for just one minute, Beck," he growled. "The world's going to be a better place without your smart-aleck mouth."

I couldn't really argue with that, so I just banged harder on the door.

"See ya," Van waved. "I'll be back to bag me a dragon."

Van walked around the train, looking at it and making sure there was no way we could get out. He then disappeared through the large hole in the moss.

"I should never have left the light on," I complained.

Kate was too worried to even say, "Told you so."

Illustration from page 67 of The Grim Knot

CHAPTER 25

The Dragon Attack

W HAT A JERK," KATE SAID, falling back into one of the padded train seats.

"A jerk is somebody who cuts you off in traffic," I told her. "He's more like a murderer."

"What a murderer," she said, correcting herself.

We had beaten and tested every bit of the train from inside, hoping to find some way out. The thick plastic windows withstood all of our kicking and hitting. I had even crawled into the engine's furnace to see if I could possibly climb out a smokestack.

Nope.

We could still hear Lizzy tearing apart everything and screaming in the back cavern. I was so mad at myself for letting Van trick me. And now he was going to steal my dragon.

As a kid, I had seen the movie *Pete's Dragon* about twenty times because I thought it was real. There's just something about a cartoon dragon that made it easy for me to suspend reality. But I remember the mousy guy with the little beard who wanted to cut the dragon up and use it for all kinds of things. Now in my mind that mousy guy and Van were one and the same.

"I bet Van doesn't even have a backpack," I growled.

Kate just shook her head.

"There's some good news," I said, trying to lighten the mood.

"Really," she said. "What?"

"I was right about Van the first time."

Kate tried to smile.

"Don't worry too much," I told her. "Maybe when he comes back, he'll let us go."

"Or maybe," she suggested, "when he returns with his tranquilizer gun he'll shoot us too."

I looked around and then repeated what I had been saying ever since I had discovered the cave. "We could start the train."

Kate closed her eyes and massaged her eyebrows.

"No, listen," I said excitedly. "We start the train and bust out of here."

"Then what?" Kate asked. "The tracks are covered with trees."

"Not the tracks on the side of the mountain," I reminded her. "They're just hidden by trees. The train will at least make it to the bottom. Somebody has to notice that."

"Nice," she said. "I'll take comfort in the fact that somebody will find our dead bodies smashed inside this train."

"Maybe that cable attached to the back will lower us slowly," I said wishfully.

Kate looked out the rear window at the huge reel of cable.

"I guess we could just wait for him to come and finish us off," I suggested.

Kate sighed. "This train probably doesn't even work."

"Well, then, let's at least try." I hopped up. "Rip all the cushions off the chairs and see if you can pull any of that rug up."

"Why?" Kate asked standing.

"We can wrap ourselves in padding so if we do crash, it won't be as bad."

Kate apparently liked that idea because she went right to it tearing up the train's insides. I threw some small pieces of cobweb-covered wood into the engine and tore off one of the seat backs. The seat backs were made of wood and had fabric covering it. I figured the fabric would be easier to get lit than the pieces of wood. I got the matches and struck one up. Luckily the train was made back in the good old days when there wasn't a lot of thought going into how flammable the material was.

The seat burst into flame and in a minute all the small pieces of wood were burning nicely. I began placing chunks of coal in the mix and soon there was a roaring fire. It was so hot the front of me was nothing but sweat now. And since we couldn't open any of the windows, the entire space was beginning to feel like an oven on steroids.

Kate continued to rip the train apart as I shoveled more and more coal into the furnace. I shut the door to let the heat build and helped Kate out. She had pulled up some long velvet rope that had lined the carpet down the aisle.

"We can sort of tie ourselves to a seat," she panted. "It'll be like a seat belt. It's really getting hot in here."

I couldn't clearly hear her because of all the sweat in my ears. I opened the furnace and shoveled more coal in. The needles on the three gauges were beginning to rise quickly. I was excited, sweaty, and frightened all at once. The engine began to make all sorts of interesting noises, reminding me of a really old man struggling to get up from a chair he had sat in for years.

"Wrap yourself up!" I yelled.

Kate had already tied herself into one of the chairs and she was shoving padding all around her. Her red hair was wet from the heat and hanging in her face.

"Tighten my straps!" she yelled.

I pulled on the velvet ropes and made sure she was nice and secure. Then I put more coal in and began to shove pillows down my pants and up my shirt.

The gauges were rising fast. On one of the smaller ones, the arrow was in the red section, and the train was beginning to shiver. I put more coal in and got my velvet rope ready. One of the gauges began to shake and whistle. I flipped a big red switch and the front train light went on, shining toward the moss wall. I grabbed the crank and looked back at Kate.

"Should I do it?" I yelled.

"No," she hollered back.

That was all I needed. I threw the crank forward and the train lurched, starting out slowly. There was only about two hundred feet of track before it reached the moss wall and started down the mountain so I hurried to my seat and tied myself in as best as possible.

The old train huffed, gaining more momentum with each turn of the wheels. It pulled out from under the metal platform.

"This is a really bad idea," Kate exclaimed.

"I know," I replied.

The huffing and puffing of the train was so strained and so jarring, I could feel it in my sweaty bones. By the time we were fifty feet away from the moss opening, we were rolling.

"We're going to die," she screamed.

"You're probably right," I screamed back. "I'm sorry for getting you into this."

"I know you are," she replied.

I looked over at Kate. She was covered with fabric and stuffing.

She looked at me. "This is probably one of the dumbest ways to die."

I couldn't argue that. We both held onto the seat backs in front of us as the train continued to pick up speed. It was only a few feet away from the moss wall now. In my mind I saw us shooting out of the green wall and blasting out over the forest. But the nose of the train just pushed the moss wall slowly out. Then there was a brief moment before the nose of the train dropped down like the front cart of a roller coaster.

I screamed my personal loudest.

The front section now pulled the rest of the train quickly out of the cave. The accordion design was brilliant, shaping the train into an arrow that was flying down the mountain. My heart had long since popped out of the top of my head, and Kate was saying things I couldn't understand in a very loud voice. The slope of the tracks was so severe that it felt like we were freefalling. I looked out the windows and watched the mountain blow by us. The top of the train was thwacking and destroying any of the sideways trees that were growing in our way.

"Beck!" Kate screamed.

"Sorry!" I apologized again.

In what seemed like one very long, frightening instant we reached the bottom of the mountain. I thought we'd just slam into the trees and be obliterated, instead the train bumped and raced along the track. The weight of it was so tremendous and the fall down the mountain had given it such speed that there was no way it was going to stop yet.

It blew through the few trees that were growing through the tracks and shredded any of those near the sides. All the rain and the still-spongy ground made the trees just pop up out of the soil.

"It's not stopping!" Kate informed me needlessly.

"We have to stop eventually," I shouted back.

Everything was happening so fast. It felt like the world was spinning at a rate far faster than it should. I could see darkness and trees and stars and bits of light from the train's lantern. We hit a big tree on the left side of the track and the train lifted a few inches and then its wheels slammed back down on the tracks. I could see sparks snapping and shooting up from below. The out-of-control train smacked another tree. It flipped up and shot back. The trunk of it pierced the roof and came shooting down between Kate and me. We both looked at the tree and screamed even louder.

I achieved a new personal best.

I felt like I was going to pass out. The velvet rope was coming loose and I was so shaken I couldn't see clearly. My head crashed into the seat back in front of me and I could feel blood beginning to trickle down from the gash.

"This . . . was . . . a . . . really . . . bad . . . idea!" I yelled.

Kate didn't have time to respond. The train slammed into the back of the garage and everything went black.

Illustration from page 70 of The Grim Knot

CHAPTER 26

Another One Bites the Dust

I HEARD THE SOUND OF WATER running and stones dropping. I opened my eyes and was surprised to discover that I wasn't dead—in fact I was fine and still tied into my seat. The train was on its side, but practically standing on its nose. I figure the ground beneath the garage had stopped it. The roof of the train was completely cracked, and there was a large part of it missing from the back. I heard Kate struggling. I turned my head to look at her. She was conscious and trying to untie the knot on her rope with her teeth. Her head was covered in dust but she looked okay. Actually she looked better than okay.

I shook off my binding and carefully climbed up the tilted seats to help Kate.

"We're alive," I said nonchalantly.

"I can't believe it," Kate puffed while holding on to the back of her seat so she didn't slide down.

"My idea worked," I pointed out.

"You call this worked?" she smiled weakly.

"What? The ground stopped us."

We both were pretty scratched up, but our bodies were still intact. I could hear the steam engine still sputtering and hissing.

"Don't move," Kate said suddenly.

I stopped moving. "Why?"

She leaned to the side to look through a busted hole. "Um, I think we're sort of hanging."

"Whaddya mean 'sort of hanging'?" I asked, moving to see what she saw.

Kate was wrong, we weren't sort of hanging, we were hanging. We had busted through the back of the garage and then angled almost straight down into a hole. The tracks actually went down deeper but we were somehow hanging. I looked toward the rear of the train. I could see the steel cable attached to the back. It was taut and keeping us from falling any farther. The rear of the train was about ten feet beneath the garage house floor. Light from the garage lamps lit the scene in an eerie glow.

"We should get out of here," Kate whispered.

"I agree," I said, being agreeable.

We climbed up the seats and then worked our way out of the hole in the roof. The huge train moaned and swayed slightly which made both of us move a little quicker. We reached the back end where the cable was attached and climbed up the sloped track. Water was running down the rails from a busted pipe in the garage floor.

We reached ground level where the tracks had once gone under the garage wall. There was no longer any wall. We stood up and dusted ourselves off while checking for any breaks or bruises.

"You just might be too exciting for me," Kate joked.

"I get that a lot," I smiled.

We looked at the section of wall we had destroyed and then gazed out toward the trees. I could see straight into the forest thanks to the path we had cleared out. It was too dark to see all the way to the mountain, but I could see the cave's entrance lit up on the side of it. The train had knocked out almost all of the moss, so it was easy to spot the large glowing hole. The long, tight cable stretched out from where I stood and ran straight up to the cave like a zip line.

Thomas and Scott came running around the far corner of the garage. Scott was carrying a shotgun, and Thomas had a closed umbrella. Scott swore as he looked at the destroyed garage wall. He slapped his forehead and began to yell at us.

"You did this?" he ranted.

"It was sort of an accident," I said lamely. "We almost died."

"Calm yourself," Thomas insisted. "Is everyone okay?"

"We're fine, but we were locked up," Kate told them. "This was the only way out."

"Is that a train engine?" Scott asked in shock as he stared down through the huge hole.

Kate and I nodded.

"You'd better fill us in, Beck," Scott insisted.

I gave both Scott and Thomas the quick, yet heavily edited, version of what had transpired. I told them about finding the cave and about Van locking us up in the train. I told them about having no other option and how we tied ourselves to the seats. I told them everything I could remember, although I might have accidentally left out the part about the dragon.

"Where's that reporter now?" Scott asked, turning his fury from me to Van.

"We don't know," I said honestly.

"The important thing is that everyone's okay," Thomas said kindly.

"Everyone's fine," I replied. "It could have been much worse."

The hanging train moaned, followed by a thunderous crack in the air. The taut cable went limp. We all stepped back as the back of the train dropped down two more floors. There was a great noise as it hit the very bottom of the tracks. We all stood there staring into the hole, listening to things break and split apart. I was pretty happy we had gotten out in time.

"Well, that's a little worse," I observed.

I was going to say more, but an ear-splitting noise rang through the air. I turned and glanced toward the mountain. A dark smear shot out of the lit-up cave. I could see Lizzy's silhouette for a second. It was enough to make all of us shiver. Scott swore again, and Thomas went weak in the knees.

"Oh yeah," I said apologetically. "And there was a dragon."

I'm not sure I've ever heard Thomas curse before.

Lizzy was temporarily lost in the darkness, but I heard her scream getting louder as she flew closer. All four of us ran toward the manor. When I passed the snake fountain I stopped and looked up. I could see Lizzy's shadow against the half moon. She twisted and dove toward the manor screeching.

Scott raised his shotgun and fired twice.

"That's no good," I yelled. "There's only one way to kill her and it isn't with a gun."

Lizzy extended her back legs down and out and then slammed into the copper dome. Her talons scraped across the metal. She stopped and began clawing at the dome, desperately trying to take hold of something. Lizzy raised her head back in a fit and blew fire up into the night like a flaming fountain.

"Aeron!" Thomas hollered. Even when he screamed, Thomas sounded like a gentleman.

The fire backlit all the gargoyles on the edge of the roof and made it look like a host of beings were looking down at us. Lizzy's talons grabbed hold of the top of the dome and she peeled back a large piece of the copper. Thomas and Scott ran toward one of the back doors of the manor. Kate started to follow, but I grabbed her arm.

"Wait!" I ordered.

"What are you doing?" she asked.

"We can't do anything about her from up there," I said frantically. "She just wants the metal. She'll return to the cave with what she's pillaged."

"So?" Kate asked.

"We've got to get to the cave and put a stop to her."

"How?"

"I don't know," I hollered. "Maybe we can lock her back up. I just know there's nothing we can do from in the dome."

"We almost died up there," Kate reminded me.

"Well, you can wait here if you want," I offered.

"No way."

We were pretty beat up. My body was growing rapidly more achy from the shock of the accident, and I had blood all over my arms. I could also feel a huge lump rising on the back of my head. Kate wasn't in much better shape, but we had no time to sit around and lick our wounds.

"Running hurts," I hollered as we ran.

"Tell me about it."

"Well, when my feet slap down on the ground, it sends shockwaves shooting up and down my entire body."

"Don't really tell me," Kate grunted.

"Oh," I puffed back.

"How do you think Lizzy got out anyway?" Kate yelled.

"I have no idea. I slid the bolt through the lock."

We couldn't run all the way to the stone stairs, but we walked as fast as possible. We watched Lizzy fly overhead as she returned to the cave to drop off some of her spoils.

"Keep going," I told Kate. "She'll probably go back for more."

We reached the stone steps and I cursed every stair I had to climb. Halfway up, we saw Lizzy burst out of the cave above and head back toward the manor.

"Hurry!" I ordered.

"I'm ten steps ahead of you," Kate yelled back.

"Well, then wait up," I pleaded.

By the time we reached the cave opening, I was totally out of breath, strength, and courage. I would have done almost anything to just sit down, rest up, and have someone else take care of the problem I created.

As I stepped into the cave I could see quite clearly how Lizzy had gotten out. The stone wall between the front cavern and the back one was broken open, right behind where the train had once sat. I could see directly into the back cavern.

"I don't think we'll be locking her up back in there," I said. "So the train broke the wall?"

"The steel cable," Kate said. "When the train fell into the garage hole it was because the reel busted away from the wall and broke open a hole for Lizzy."

I could see the huge wide reel standing up on its side near the front of the metal platform the train had once been parked under. The reel was taller than the platform. There was tangled cable lying across the floor in large, messy coils.

"So what do we do?" Kate asked desperately. "We can't lock her up, and what's Lizzy going to do after she gets all of the copper dome?"

"Probably head into Kingsplot," I said.

"You've got to kill her," Kate said solemnly. "Seriously, Beck."

"I know," I replied mournfully.

"So do you jab a stick in her throat like the last ones?"

"No," I answered. "There's only one way to kill her."

"How?"

"We've got to choke her."

Kate laughed. "You're kidding, right?"

I shook my head.

"You can't choke her," Kate yelled. "She's huge."

"I was supposed to do it right after she was born," I explained.

"But you didn't."

"I'm perfectly aware of that," I argued.

"So what now?"

I probably would have said something brilliant if it had not been for the interruption of Lizzy. We heard her scream first and then like a big wad of scary, she entered the cave. Kate and I hid behind the huge reel.

Lizzy had another copper section in her talons. She dropped her spoils and folded her rubbery wings. The gray stripes on her body were spreading, making her bottom half almost completely dark. She rocked back and forth on her feet and then blew fire while rotating her head. The flames vanished, and she screamed as if she were the queen of the world. Lizzy leaned her head down and picked up the copper roof with her mouth. We watched her carry it through the hole in the wall and back toward her nest.

"Okay," I whispered. "She'll probably go back for the rest of the dome. So we should have a plan to take care of her when she returns."

Lizzy came out of the back, ran to the moss opening, and dived out into the dark.

"There's only one thing we can do," Kate said. "We've got to get her into that cage when she gets back."

"She won't go in there," I argued.

"Maybe with some bait she will. You could stand in the cage, and when she goes in, I will shut the door and you'll slip right out the bars. But you've just got to stay in there long enough for me to get the bars closed."

I didn't like the plan for a whole bunch of reasons, but the most concerning one was me being the bait. Unfortunately, I couldn't think of a better one.

"What if she doesn't come to me?" I asked. "She's pretty focused on pillaging."

Kate had a solution for that too. We ran through the broken wall and up to the pile of organ pipes. I gazed down into the hole Lizzy had made for a nest and saw a single stone.

I pointed and stuttered at the same time.

"It's just a rock, right?" Kate asked, worried.

"I don't think so."

"I thought she couldn't produce a stone until she was killed," Kate said.

"The queen's different," I moaned. "That stone produces a king."

"How do you know?"

"It was in the book," I said dejectedly.

"Well, let's deal with one thing at a time," Kate insisted. "You've got to get into that cage!"

Kate had me drag one of the organ pipes into the cage with me. She then positioned herself behind some cereal drums as I stood shakily inside the large cage holding up the pipe. I kept my eyes closed and my ears open. When I heard Lizzy's far cry my eyelids shot open and my arms began to imitate my shaking knees.

I heard Lizzy land and drop her spoils in the front of the cave. I heard her wings flap twice and then suddenly she was coming through the hole in the wall with a mouthful of roof. I leaned on the pipe to keep myself from falling over.

Lizzy stepped up to her nest and dropped the roof on top of the pile of pillaged goods. Instantly I could tell she was ill at ease because she began to bristle and look around frantically. She obviously figured out one of her pipes was missing.

She spotted me holding her possession.

"Yeah, that's right," I said, talking big. "I've got your precious pipe."

Lizzy snorted, and my stomach scrambled to hide behind my lungs.

"Come get it, Lizzy," I hollered. I knocked on the pipe with my knuckles.

She roared and began to step in my direction.

"Seriously," I told her. "If you can take it from me, it's all yours."

Lizzy lowered her head and stomped faster. I backed up until I couldn't back up any further. She stopped about ten feet in front of the cage and clawed at the dirt.

"Come on," I challenged.

Lizzy screamed and whipped her tail violently against the ground. Her face and body were amazing. Her horns were pure white and her blue eyes were now circled by gray scales. She was even larger than she had been yesterday, and I wished so badly that she was still as kind to me as she once had been. I saw no kindness in her eyes.

"Don't stop now," I ordered.

She stepped halfway through the large door and snorted wickedly.

"You don't seem very committed to this pipe," I told her. "I mean you're moving pretty slow."

Lizzy stepped in further. She looked at me with her huge eyes. I thought for a second that she was going to smile and it would be a happy ending, but instead she opened her jaws as large as she could and lunged toward me screaming.

I screamed too, throwing the pipe at her and dashing around her right front leg. I could see Kate running to close the cage door as Lizzy's tail whipped me off of my feet and sent me flying into the dirt. I got to my feet just as she turned around. I could hear her scream, and I felt fire pushing up against my back.

Kate slammed the cage door and put the pin in it. Kate's actions distracted Lizzy and I slipped through the bars.

"You're on fire!" Kate screamed.

I ran ten feet and dived to the dirt to roll around a little. The small flames on my back were quickly extinguished. Kate ran to me and helped me sit up.

"Are you okay?" she asked with such concern that I felt I should milk it a little.

"Fine," I coughed.

Lizzy was not happy. She was pulling at the bars with her talons and flapping her wings like a spoiled dragon.

"I can't believe we did it!" I yelled. "I can't believe it!"

"Nor can I," a voice said from behind us.

I turned my head so quickly it almost snapped off.

"Whitey," I said in shock.

Whitey was wearing his brown robe with the hood pulled down over his eyes. He waved his white hands around and even in the bad lighting they seemed to glow.

"Congratulations, Beck," he said kindly. "You're a truly brave soul." Kate cleared her throat. "And you as well, young lady."

"Lizzy's still not dead," I reminded him. "But I just thought of something as she was trying to kill me. I guess almost dying kinda clears my mind. I was thinking that if she can only die by being choked, and if she's growing so fast, maybe the rope around her neck will just become so tight she'll choke to death."

"Perhaps," Whitey said slowly. "But that's leaving much to chance. It might be best if we take care of it sooner. Fetch me some rope."

I turned and looked around the cavern.

"Um, Beck," Kate whispered from the side of her mouth. "Can I talk to you?"

"Let's get that rope first." I pointed to a large coil.

Kate was jogging right behind me trying to tell me something. "Are you sure you can trust this guy?"

"No," I said. "But if he's willing to help us, I'll be glad to let him."

I grabbed the lengthy coil of rope and threw it over my right shoulder. As I turned around, I thought my eyes were playing tricks on me. Whitey was pulling the pin out of the cage door and the door was swinging open.

"What are you doing?!" I yelled.

"What I was born to do," he laughed.

Lizzy stomped out of the cage and gazed directly at me.

"She'll kill me," I argued, as if he didn't know that already.

Whitey just stared at me. My only chance was to run for it. I looked at Kate.

"Go," I screamed.

Kate took off, and I dropped the rope and dashed madly for the hole in the wall. Kate tripped, and I grabbed her hand and pulled her up. I could hear Lizzy gliding toward us screeching. We scrambled through the hole as Lizzy plowed into the back of us sending Kate and I flying in two different directions. Kate was tossed toward the metal door and I landed hard under the metal train platform. My right arm smacked one of the steel beams.

I tried to scream gracefully.

Lizzy stood on her hind legs and exhaled. As she breathed out, fire filled the room and I was afraid I was going to melt right where I was. She slammed her front legs down and stomped closer to me as I writhed in pain. I wanted to cross my hands and call a time-out, but my right arm was hurt, and I didn't think Lizzy was the kind of dragon who played by those rules.

Kate was up and throwing rocks at the back of Lizzy.

"Over here!" she yelled.

Lizzy had no interest in Kate. She stepped even closer to me.

"Stop it!" Kate kept screaming. "Stop!"

Lizzy stepped past the huge reel and over some of the tangled cable that was attached to it. As one of her back feet came down it became caught in the cable, tethering her where she was. She flapped her wings and pulled her leg up violently. As she yanked herself forward, the cable moved and shifted. I turned my head and saw that the huge iron reel was beginning to roll slowly as Lizzy struggled.

Lizzy gave up on her trapped leg and turned her focus back on me. She dragged the tangled cable, screaming. The steel cable was wound through one of the metal beams that held up the platform above me. Each step Lizzy took moved the cable and caused the reel to roll away from us.

My arm hurt horribly and blood from my forehead was dripping into my eyes. I was seeing red.

"Lizzy!" I heard Kate scream.

Lizzy looked at me and smiled. Sadly, it wasn't the kind

of smile I was hoping to see from her. Instead it was the kind of smile that caused my entire body to go cold and my soul to look for a way out of my doomed body.

"Kate!" I yelled, knowing she couldn't do anything.

I was in the process of saying good-bye to my life when Kate threw a loop of rope around Lizzy's head and pulled back to tighten it.

"Hold on, Beck!"

I could see Kate straining as if playing tug-of-war with Lizzy's neck. Unfortunately, I could also tell that Kate wasn't nearly strong enough to deliver a complete strangling. It was enough, however, to cause Lizzy to pay some attention to Kate instead of me.

I watched Kate pull on the rope, and I saw the tangled wire that Lizzy was standing in. The big reel that had the end of the wire still hooked to it was rolling further away as Lizzy moved. My mind kept telling me that there was something I should be aware of and doing, but I couldn't focus on it.

Lizzy screeched and shuffled, tangling her feet in the wire even more. It then became clear to me what I had to do.

"Thank you, Professor Squall," I whispered.

I flipped over onto my stomach and crawled to the steel beam with the metal rungs. I lifted a section of the wire cable over my shoulder and pulled myself up on the rungs. My right arm hurt so badly it was hard to use it much.

Kate screamed at Lizzy and tugged on the rope.

I whimpered and wailed as I pulled myself up the ladder. The steel cable was so heavy I thought the weight of it was going to cut me in half. I got to the top of the platform and crawled up, crying in pain. With my right leg and left arm I hoisted the loop of cable on top of the platform and around the top of one of the beams. As I got it into place, my left leg slipped and I fell back to the ground in a heap of misery and pain.

I looked over at Kate and was surprised to see Van standing over her with a shovel. He swung the shovel, and Kate flew to the ground. I watched her slide across the ground and then just lay there.

"Kate!" I yelled.

Both Lizzy and Van turned to look at me.

"Stop!" I begged.

"I followed you back up here," Van said. "I heard the train crashing through the woods. You almost hit me."

"I'd feel bad about that," I said, "but you left us for dead."

"Small price to pay for fame," he crowed creepily. "You can't kill the dragon! She must live."

Van's sentiment was nice, but apparently Lizzy didn't feel the same way about him. She opened her mouth and roared.

Then she swung her head down, and with one swift snap of her jaws, Van was gone. He just vanished. I couldn't believe my eyes—but where my eyes might have been fooled, my stomach wasn't. I leaned to my right and lost my lunch, dinner, and any snacks I might have had in between. I couldn't do this anymore. Kate wasn't moving, Van was gone, and my body ached like an overbeaten piñata.

Lizzy swallowed, raised her head up, and blew fire into the air. She then lowered her head and glared directly at me with her dark blue eyes. She shuffled closer to me. I looked at the moving cable I had strung around the top of the platform. The reel was rolling directly toward the moss opening.

"Come on!" I yelled. "Aren't you going to finish me off?"

Lizzy lunged at me but her tangled foot made her fall forward. Her huge head hit the ground and she slid to a stop a couple of feet away. It was just what I needed. I sprang up and lifted a loop of the cable over Lizzy's head. She pushed herself up onto her back legs ranting and writhing, the cable slipping down around her neck. She attacked again, and the reel rolled closer to the exit.

My brain belched and shivered as a small bit of hope covered my heart.

"I'm so sorry, Lizzy," I whimpered.

Lizzy screamed and I crawled backward, dragging myself as

far from her as I could. I got about ten feet away before the wall stopped me. She stood all the way up and tried to get closer, but the cable around her neck and foot made it very difficult for her to move. Kate was still lying lifeless on the ground.

The dragon stepped closer. Smoke was puffing from her nostrils, and her blue eyes looked red. The mammoth reel was still rolling toward the exit, but it was going slower than I needed it to.

"Come and get me!" I cried. "You crazy lizard!"

Lizzy dug all four feet into the ground and plunged forward three feet. The reel began to roll faster; the pulley I created with the steel beams was working perfectly.

"Come on," I hollered. "Is that all you've got!"

Lizzy opened her mouth and screamed like a choir full of banshees. Dragon spit and phlegm sprayed all over me. She threw her front legs forward and with amazing strength moved to within a couple of feet of me. I could see the reel moving, but I knew it was too late. Lizzy stood up on her hind legs and reached her front ones out as if measuring the distance between her and me. She leaned her long neck back and then swung her head forward. I saw her sharp wet teeth flying toward me, and I knew it was over. I closed my eyes waiting to hear the sound of my skull crunching. Instead, all I heard was the noise of something gargantuan falling just outside of the cave.

I opened my eyes.

Lizzy's mouth was moving away from me, and her eyes were wide with surprise. I looked over to see the reel, and it was gone. It had rolled right out of the cave with the end of the cable attached to it. The cable whizzed around the metal beam I had looped it over. The loose coil wrapped around Lizzy's neck tightened and pulled her up. She was flipped onto her back, and then with one fantastic tug, the cable completely drew in and constricted with a deadly grip around Lizzy's neck. The queen looked at me with her blue eyes as she choked and emitted her final breath. She was thoroughly and completely choked.

I got up onto my knees and used my one good arm to crawl over to Kate. I think I was crying, but there was so much blood and sweat on my face it was kind of hard to tell. Kate was still breathing, and as I leaned my face over hers she opened her blue eyes.

"You're alive," I exclaimed.

"I think you're right," she groaned, "but my head hurts."

"I think my arm's broken," I told her.

We helped each other up. We leaned against one another and looked at Lizzy. Her body began to spark and break up, and then, like the other dragons before it, it broke into a billion pieces and dissolved. There was nothing left but a tangled mess of cable.

"I can't believe it," I smiled. "Professor Squall's lecture on simple machinery paid off."

"I'm sure he'd be proud," she said.

"Lizzy was amazing," I mourned.

"Yeah," Kate said quietly. "But now we need a doctor."

Kate helped me make a sling for my arm out of my jacket so the hike down the stairs wouldn't be as painful. It wasn't a half-bad sling considering it was made from a plastic windbreaker.

We were walking toward the exit when I remembered the stone. "Wait," I said. "What happened to Whitey? And we need that stone."

"We'll get it later," Kate insisted.

"No, we can't leave it."

The two of us walked over the crumbled rock from the hole in the cave and back toward the nest. When we reached it, I looked down.

"Is it me?" Kate asked worriedly. "Or is there no stone?"

"He took it," I cried.

I could see that the back tunnel door was open. Whitey had taken the rock and ran, and I was in no mood to start exploring the dark tunnel to look for him. I groaned mournfully.

"You know what?" Kate asked me.

"What?"

"I know it sounds weird, but think I might know where he went."

I looked at her like she was crazy. "Does it involve going down that tunnel?"

She shook her head.

"Then let's go."

Kate took my hand and pulled me quickly toward the exit and down the stairs. Even in the dark we could see the enormous reel that had rolled out of the cave and whose great weight had helped strangle Lizzy. It was hanging by the cable halfway down the side of the mountain.

Kate told me where she thought Whitey had gone as we walked through the dark trees. She also told me why she thought Whitey had gone there. I wanted to disagree with her, but I had no theories of my own. The one thing I did know was that before we did anything else, I needed to talk to my dad.

Illustration from page 77 of The Grim Knot

CHAPTER 27

Was It All Worth It?

THE MANOR WAS SHROUDED IN BLACK. Only the lamp that hung above the wide service entry was diligent enough to keep shining. Inside, the kitchen was dark, and there was no sign of Millie and anyone else.

"Where is everybody?" Kate asked.

"I'm sure they're out looking for us," I said, trying to comfort myself.

The emptiness of the manor made me uneasy. I mean, I was used to it being vacant and lonely, but the silence after what had just happened didn't seem right. I picked up the phone and made a quick call.

"What if your dad's gone too?" Kate asked.

"I guess we'll find that out in a minute," I answered.

We hiked up the stairs. I was so sick of steps I felt like

puking. Of course it could have also been that I was just in the mood to throw up.

"If I ever inherit this place, the first thing I'm doing is putting in an elevator," I complained.

"Sounds like a good idea," Kate gasped.

When we got to the top the door was open, and I could see that the dome roof was almost completely gone. I entered and reached for the light switch. Wind was dipping in and stringing itself around like toilet paper. The dome room was in a lot more ruin than the last time the dragons had been out.

My father was standing in the middle of the room with his arms behind his back and his face looking up toward the stars. Light from the open door painted the space and cast long shadows on anything in the room. My father's ragged hair and shirt fluttered like ribbons on a running fan.

"Dad," I whispered, my voice competing with the soft wind.

He didn't answer.

"It's me, Beck," I clarified.

"I saw the dragon," he said quietly, never taking his eyes off of the stars.

"Yeah," I replied, feeling incredibly guilty. "Sorry about the roof."

Kate was right behind me. She nudged my back.

"Dad?"

"Yes," he answered.

"She's gone," I reported.

"I figured," he sighed.

Kate nudged me again. I decided to just get her dumb idea out of the way.

"You left us for dead," I told him.

My father turned his head and looked at me and then Kate. He looked back up at the stars, his hands still clasped behind his back. It was hard to tell, but he appeared to be trembling just a bit.

"I had her locked up, and you let her go," I said sadly. "You're Whitey."

"Lies," my father snapped.

"Dad."

"I don't know what you're talking about," he insisted.

I could tell by the way my father was talking that he was lying.

"You tricked me into planting that stone."

"No, I did not."

"You knew I wouldn't kill it when it was young," I went on. "You don't really want this to end. And you took the stone."

For a second my father was silent, and I thought he was going to tell me I was wrong. Instead he turned and began to frantically rant.

"You don't understand! These are dragons!" he pleaded. "They're in our blood. I couldn't find the stone on my own, and I had to see one again."

"So, you put on a bunch of white makeup, wear glasses and a robe, and talk like a different person?" I asked. "I should have figured it out myself. I guess I just never in my wildest dreams thought you would try to trick me. Kate recognized you."

My father's body shook even harder.

"It's my fault," I told him. "You kept yourself up here all those years to break the family cycle and I came along and messed things up. If you had never seen a dragon, you would have been fine. Well, not fine, but . . . well, you would have just been a misunderstood hermit."

"I must stop you," he said.

I looked around. "Stop me from what?"

"You're a Pillage," he whispered. "And you're going to destroy it all. The dragons are a protection and our gift."

"The dragons are our curse," I reminded him. "Remember?"

My father reached behind a chest of drawers and pulled out the same sword he had flashed me with in the hospital. I should have been frightened, but my mind was preoccupied with thinking about how he actually had visited me when I was in the hospital. I would have been touched, but he was already touched enough for the both of us.

He held the sword halfway up and gazed at me. Even in the low light I could see the confusion and darkness in his eyes.

"Dad," I pleaded.

He blinked and then dropped the sword. His body began to twitch as he let go of his emotions and started to sob. I stepped up and put my one good arm around him. I could feel Kate's hand on my shoulder as she was doing her best to be supportive of me and my messed-up home life.

"I told you I was sick," my father said mournfully.

"I thought you were talking about me," I replied.

"It's not always about you," Kate whispered. She needed to work on her support skills a little more.

"Don't worry," I told my dad. "We'll get you help."

As if on cue, Sheriff Pax climbed up into the dome. There was another officer and a woman with him.

I was so glad he had taken my call seriously.

Illustration from page 79 of The Grim Knot

CHAPTER 28

Flash

THE SUN FELT MAGNIFICENT on my arms and neck. It was a clear day and the tiny bit of wind felt like a cool reminder that I was both alive and outdoors. From where I was sitting I could see forever, or at least all of the Hagen Valley and the mountains that surrounded it. I was sitting on top of the dome hammering the last pieces of roof for the repair. Wyatt and Kate were both helping me out.

"After this, Scott wants us to start on the garage repairs," I said.

"Us?" Kate asked.

I looked at her and smiled. She was so pretty. She was wearing jeans and a green T-shirt. Her dark red hair and blue eyes drove me crazy.

"Would you two get a roof," Wyatt said, trying to be funny.

We both just stared at him.

"What?" he asked. "That was pretty good. I mean we're on a roof."

We laughed at him and I continued pounding nails.

Kate picked up another piece of the copper roofing and as she moved it, light flashed off it, blinding me for a moment.

I could see images in the flash of light.

I could see my father. He was checked into the hospital in Kingsplot and was being taken care of by well-trained people like Nurse Agatha. I had visited him every day and he was making progress. He had filled me in on how he had tried to find the stone himself, and, when he couldn't, a part of him began taking on the personality of Whitey. He claimed to not even remember letting the dragon out of the cage or any of our conversations. He had moved to the cavern through the hidden trap door in the dome and through a tunnel that ran all the way over and up to the back cavern. He was quick to say he would be all the way better soon, but part of me knew he would never be himself completely until there was no stone left.

In that flash I also saw the stone.

I had found it in a trunk in the dome where my father kept his possessions. It wasn't a very good hiding place, but it was the best he could do in his state of mind. I took it out and placed it somewhere much better, hoping I wouldn't have to see it for a long time, but knowing sooner or later I would. I was, after all, a Pillage.

The reason Millie, Wane, and Scott had been missing was because they had taken Wane to the emergency room. While Lizzy had been tearing apart the dome roof they had all gotten scraped up and Wane had received a concussion from a falling board. None of them said a thing about dragons. We had all been through enough, and there didn't seem to be any wisdom in making things worse. Thomas had been missing because he had actually gone out into the forest looking for me and Kate.

Kate moved another piece of roof, and a second flash brought me out of my thoughts. I could clearly see every nail and plank we still needed to work on to completely repair the dome. It reminded me of my family and all the work that was still needed to repair my family and my father. For some reason the work didn't scare me.

"You're not hammering," Wyatt complained.

Millie came out from beneath the dome and onto the seventh-floor terrace. She had a tray full of food and drinks.

"Are you three hungry?" she hollered up. "I've got roasted steak and cheese sandwiches, pints of raspberry lemonade, and chocolate cheesecake salad."

"That's the kind of salad I like," Wyatt joked.

I missed Lizzy. I missed the feeling of strength she gave me.

But Lizzy had taught me something. In fact, I sort of felt like her, but in reverse—she had started out kind and beautiful and grown into an ugly evil creature. Me? I was trying to pull off just the opposite. Even bigger than that was the lesson I had learned from Professor Squall. Apparently there were some things I needed to learn from grown-ups.

Kate smiled at me and handed me a sandwich.

We ate near-perfect food on a near-perfect dome during a near-perfect day. Yes, I worried about my dad, and, yes, I still had a ton of makeup homework to do, but for the moment, my life was pretty close to perfect—quixotic even.

About the Author

O BERT SKYE LOVES DRAGONS. He wishes he had a few. Actually, he wishes he had a few dozen. Unfortunately, at the moment he doesn't even have one. Because of this he's really enjoyed telling the tale of Beck Pillage and his family's ability. To quote Obert, "Dragon drool aside, writing this book has been one exciting ride." Aside from issuing quotes for the back of book jackets, Obert is also the award-winning author of the bestselling *Leven Thumps* series. Obert currently lives indoors and near a thin, winding road.